"Why did you touch me that way?"

"I don't know," Cat said, backing away. "I think I should go."

"Why did you touch me that way?" Jessica asked again, her voice soft with desire, her body burning with love and fever. "You can't shock me, Cat. Tell me."

"I — you kissed me and . . . I — it felt right."

"It felt right to me, too," Jessica whispered. "Every part of me thought it felt right." She stood between Cat and the door, so close to Cat that her breasts almost brushed Cat's folded arms.

Cat swayed slightly. "I don't know what to do, Jessica."

Jessica decided to risk everything. "Do whatever you feel is right. If you leave I won't follow you. I'll wait for you to come back. If you stay. . . ." She swallowed and couldn't go on. Her mouth was dry with want and fear, her throat tight with the words of love she longed to say.

Cat dropped her arms. "Tell me what to do," she whispered, her eyes glazed.

"No. You decide what you want to do," Jessica said in a low, intense voice. "It's your life. Your choice. Never let us misunderstand that."

WRITING AS KARIN KALLMAKER:

One Degree of Separation
Maybe Next Time
Substitute for Love
Frosting on the Cake
Unforgettable
Watermark
Making Up for Lost Time
Embrace in Motion
Wild Things
Painted Moon
Car Pool
Paperback Romance
Touchwood
In Every Port
All the Wrong Places (2004)
Sugar (2004)

WRITING AS LAURA ADAMS:

Christabel

The Tunnel of Light Trilogy:
Sleight of Hand
Seeds of Fire

Daughters of Pallas:
Night Vision
The Dawning

In Every Port

by

Karin Kallmaker

Bella
BOOKS
2003

Bella Books, Inc.
P.O. Box 10543
Tallahassee, FL 32302

First published 1989 by Naiad Press

Printed in the United States of America on acid-free paper
First Edition

Editor: Katherine V. Forrest
Cover designer: Bonnie Liss (Phoenix Graphics)

ISBN 1-931513-36-8

For February Maria,
For Always, who has tried with limited success to teach me something
useful about comma splices.

The First is for Filling Up

About the Author

Karin Kallmaker was born in 1960 and raised by her loving, middle-class parents in California's Central Valley. The physician's Statement of Live Birth plainly declares, "Sex- Female" and "Cry: Lusty." Both are still true.

From a normal childhood and equally unremarkable public school adolescence, she went on to obtain an ordinary Bachelor's degree from the California State University at Sacramento. At the age of 16, eyes wide open, she fell into the arms of her first and only sweetheart.

Ten years later, after seeing the film *Desert Hearts*, her sweetheart descended on the Berkeley Public Library determined to find some of "those" books. "Rule, Jane" led to "Lesbianism - Fiction" and then on to book after self-affirming book by and about lesbians. These books were the encouragement Karin needed to forget the so-called "mainstream" and spin her first romance for lesbians. That manuscript became her first novel, *In Every Port*. She now lives in the San Francisco Bay Area with that very same sweetheart; she is a one woman woman. The happily-ever-after couple became Mom and Moogie to Kelson in 1995 and Eleanor in 1997. They celebrate their twenty-seventh anniversary in 2004.

Karin also writes as Laura Adams, her science fiction and fantasy persona.

ONE
Whirlwind

"Thanks for thinking of me. No, nothing planned, I'm delighted to fill in. I'll make my reservations immediately. Thank you again." Jessica hung up and flipped the calendar on her desk back to April 14. The day was turning out to be much busier than she had planned.

"Book flight. Pack." She stopped writing, pencil poised. "They're fixing the hotel. Return library books. Cancel week's appointments."

She jumped when the phone rang again, then listened patiently to the pleasant and official voice. She gasped and grabbed her calendar as if it would save her. "What do you mean escrow's closing tomorrow? You said another two weeks!"

"We thought you'd be happy to hear the news. We assumed you were anxious to move into your new residence," the pleasant voice told her.

Jessica reminded "them" that "we had agreed escrow would close two weeks ago" and that "we had also decided last week it would take another two weeks to close."

"We are aware of that. We expect your closing payment within three days to avoid additional escrow fees," the voice said emotionlessly, the same way disembodied official voices say Have a nice day.

"Isn't there any way you can wait until Monday? I'm leaving on business tomorrow, probably in the afternoon."

"We can wait indefinitely, but the fees will be added on Thursday."

She asked how much the penalties were and with a gulp told the voice she would be in as soon as possible to close. Yes, she would bring a cashier's check.

She cradled her head in her hands for a few moments. Her ability to plan had always been a source of personal pride, but she hadn't planned for a delay in escrow. Why, oh why, she wailed to Herself, had the call to fill in for someone in Chicago come exactly two minutes before the call from the bank?

Assertiveness basics for women managers was her favorite topic, even after almost eight years of lecturing. But she wouldn't have agreed to go to

Chicago if she'd known escrow was going to close. On top of the hassle, the penalties were going to eat into her fee for speaking. And there was no way she was going to call and cancel Chicago — not after she'd given her verbal commitment.

She looked at her list and added "call landlord." Taking several deep breaths first, she slowly dialed her travel agent's number. If she was speaking all day Wednesday and Thursday she wanted to be in Chicago by 11 p.m. San Francisco time. That made departure sometime between four and six tomorrow afternoon, leaving her roughly twenty-four hours to move. No, she just couldn't manage, she decided.

She booked her flight and then dialed her landlord, refusing to think about the money she was going to lose in penalties. At least she wouldn't have to pay another month's rent. At least, she *thought* she wouldn't have to pay another month's rent. The management representative's voice was very friendly, yet official. Living in a modern building had benefits. The down side was the professional management company which didn't bend rules.

"We have you down as requesting an option for move-out at the end of the month. But you had to let us know last Thursday if you wanted to exercise the option or pay another month's rent." The management company had a very pleasant voice.

"That's only two working days. I'll be out by next Tuesday."

"We're sorry, but the deadline we agreed to for notice was last Thursday." The management company was very pleasant, but firm.

"If I had called you last Thursday when would I have to be out?"

3

"This Thursday."

Jessica groaned inside. If only the stupid bank had called two minutes earlier! The Chicago job was going to cost her penalties from the escrow company and another month's rent — almost double the speaking fee.

"I'll be out Thursday," she said weakly. It was impossible, but she'd manage, somehow.

"We usually suggest a tenant take at least two weeks to coordinate the entire relocation process."

"I'll be out by Thursday. Thank you for your help."

"Have a nice day," the management company said.

Jessica hung up quickly. "I'll have any goddamn kind of day I like!" she said explosively. She gave the phone a thump with her fist for good measure.

Okay, stupid, she told Herself crossly, you said you'd be out in two days, so how are you going to manage? Herself replied that she didn't know, but she'd die trying. Sometimes she hated Herself.

Figuring she wasn't going to need her March 1978 calendar page anymore, she tore it out and made another list, reminding Herself of all the reasons she was moving. She wrote them up neatly:

- No more tripping over the sofa to get to the kitchen.
- No more putting the coffee table on the sofa when you do sit-ups.
- No more sleeping and working in the same room, or using your bed for a desk.
- No more dark living room and even darker bedroom.

- No more paying absolutely the highest income tax possible.
- You deserve it!

She felt much better seeing the positive aspects in black and white. She decided she'd keep reciting them over and over to boost her morale. She took a deep breath and rolled up her sleeves. Nothing's impossible, she told Herself cheerfully.

On the one hand, almost everything was packed and labelled. She'd been expecting to move last week. Her clothes needed to be packed and her toiletries were waiting until the last minute. To hell with her cleaning deposit, there was no way she'd have the time.

She made a new list. April 1978 was almost over, so she used that page for the new list: call bank, call escrow, call movers. Pack for trip. Pack for moving. Go to bank, go to escrow, go to movers. Go to condo. Label doors for movers. Go to airport.

Piece of cake.

* * * * *

The next morning, Jessica tried to look cool and professional. Usually her navy blue suit, white blouse and pearls would look professional, especially combined with her classic navy pumps and simple, short, no-nonsense hairstyle. But the overall effect was somewhat hampered by the large box she was precariously balancing on the ledge at the teller's window.

"What — oh, yes, a cashier's check payable to the

escrow company," she said, catching the box before it slid off the ledge.

"You must be buying," the teller said conversationally as she waited for a supervisor to initial the request. "Lucky you."

"I feel pretty lucky, I guess," Jessica said. She liked her bank because the tellers were so friendly. She'd been banking there so long she knew almost everyone by name.

"I wish my husband and I could afford to buy something, but it's impossible. The interest rates are killing everyone." The teller shrugged and left to type up the check. When she came back she had a brochure. "We're installing these new automated teller machines. With one of these cards you can get cash and make deposits twenty-four hours a day. If you fill out this application, we'll send you a card. The card's free."

"Does that mean I can't come to you for help?" Jessica wasn't sure she wanted to trust her banking to a machine.

"Oh no, they're just for your convenience. We're the first to get these machines, but they'll be all over in a few years, you'll see. Sign here, and here, and the money's all yours," the teller instructed.

"I'll send in this form," Jessica said with a laugh. "But no machine is going to be as friendly as you all are."

Several of the other tellers looked up from their work and agreed noisily. "Ms. Brian is buying a condo," her teller informed them all.

Jessica flushed as all the tellers wished her well. Her spirits took a soar upward. It was nice to know personal service and friendliness still existed. The guard opened the door for her on her way out.

She felt a hell of a lot better. She virtually bounced down the street, in spite of the heavy box. Inside the box were miscellaneous household essentials she thought she'd need in her new home: tissues, toilet paper, a can of soda, an ice cube tray, scotch tape and paper and other odds and ends.

She walked the three blocks from her bank to the escrow office, shifting the box from shoulder to shoulder, ignoring the strange glances from other people — her mood was too good to be spoiled by anyone today. She was going to get moved and not pay penalties or extra rent. She, Jessica Brian, had overcome the difficulties fate had put in her path.

Then someone jostled her and the box tumbled off her shoulder onto the ground. No one stopped to help her retrieve the roll of toilet paper which had sprung loose. With a choice four-letter word, she knelt on her hands and knees and scrabbled up her belongings. As she righted herself and stood up, someone had the nerve to hand her a flyer extolling the virtues of the Briggs petition drive. Briggs could ruin anyone's day. She crammed the flyer in the box after she retrieved the roll of toilet paper. Herself devoutly hoped Jessica didn't meet anyone she knew.

"Someday I'm going to laugh like hell about all this," she muttered as she hoisted the box onto her shoulder again.

At the escrow office she had to wait for the escrow officer to finish with the current customer, so she sank down onto an uncomfortable waiting room chair and tried to catch her breath while she rubbed her shoulder.

7

She'd been waiting for a condo in a cut-up Victorian to become available for almost three years. She knew of people who'd waited for six or seven years, but that was the extreme in San Francisco. She was glad waiting had taken as long as it had. Now she was in a stronger financial position because of some hard, non-stop work. What with the sixteen percent interest rate on her mortgage, she needed every penny she could get together for a down-payment.

The last twelve years had been hard work, but work was everything. With her parents dying when she was nineteen and leaving her with only her own resources to guide her, she had pursued a business degree, then her MBA. And ever since she had discovered she enjoyed public speaking, she'd been laboring to get her name known on the circuit, working to bring assertiveness out of the dark ages and make business people realize it wasn't just a fancy word for "aggressive" — or, when men applied it to women, "bitchy."

"Ms. Brian? This way, please."

The pleasant voice belonged to a pleasant woman who, in an accordingly pleasant manner, began going through the papers and waivers and affidavits and notes and statements of escrow. Reviewing the paperwork took far longer than Jessica had thought it would, but she finally signed on the last dotted line.

"And here are your keys, Ms. Brian. We're so pleased to have done business with you." The woman smiled pleasantly as she handed over a small envelope. Jessica smiled back pleasantly and said how glad she was to have done business with "them." She

8

hated it when companies forgot they were people, and they forgot their customers were people, too.

Vince, President and Founder of Vince's Rapid Move, grinned cheekily at her and took a key and her list of instructions.

"No problem, lady, we'll leave the old apartment key at the office and push the key to the condo under the door when we're through. We'll be done on Wednesday, no problem. We do rush jobs all the time."

"I've marked all the boxes and the rooms will be marked."

"No problem, we do this kind of stuff all the time."

"Thank you." As Jessica walked back to the street to hail a cab to her new home, the box balanced on the other shoulder, she tried to shake her uneasy feeling.

But the last twenty-four hours seemed almost worth the hassle when she unlocked the building door and then took the old-fashioned cage elevator three floors to the top. There were two doors across from each other in the little lobby on the third floor. The one to the left was all hers — and the mortgage company's. She'd never been to her new home alone, only with the real estate agent. She turned the key and opened the door. She wandered from room to room, sighing with delight.

The joyful completion she felt had been a long time coming. She had put work before play insistently, single-mindedly. And now she had her own

9

place, big enough so the sofa, bed and desk weren't all in the same cramped room. There was enough space for her books and her records and her new VCR. Enough room to do sit-ups without having to move the coffee table. Enough room to live, finally. With a giggle of sheer happiness, she threw out her arms and twirled around the living room like Julie Andrews on the mountaintop at the beginning of *The Sound of Music.*

She went around and hung signs for the movers: BEDROOM, OFFICE, DESK HERE, ENTERTAIN-MENT CENTER HERE, and so on. The place shouldn't be too bad when she got back, provided they could read English. She put the roll of toilet paper on its holder, the paper towels in the kitchen, the soda in the refrigerator, and then filled the ice tray. When she got back on Friday there would at least be something cold to drink.

She was left with an empty box, except for the political flyer. She had ceased to be interested in politics when Richard Nixon had thumbed his nose at the Constitution and received an unconditional pardon for his deeds. Jimmy Carter seemed like a very nice man. At least he believed in human rights.

But this petition drive was for a proposal sponsored by State Senator John Briggs to save the country's children by barring any homosexual person from teaching in public schools. The mere idea frightened and angered her at the same time. She shredded the flyer and decided to forget about it. She knew it was easy to forget about things which made you angry and frightened if you'd had a lot of practice.

She locked the door and went down to the manager's office, found out about the mail, how she paid the residents' association fees, and listened to a variety of rules about stereos and so on. Glancing at her watch in sudden alarm, she said goodbye to the manager and dashed out the building door. There was a muffled exclamation and Jessica realized her impetuous exit had almost knocked someone over.

"Oh my gosh, I'm so sorry. Here, let me hold the door for you. I usually look where I'm going," Jessica explained. She could only see the top of a blonde head and two brown eyes behind two large grocery bags. "Can I help you?"

"No," the woman gasped, "I do this all the time." The woman hupped the bags up once and Jessica noticed the strong hands and arms gripping the bags. They seemed out of proportion with the woman's petiteness. Letting the door close, Jessica registered the brown eyes, which had either been sparkling with annoyance or laughter, and dashed for the bus.

Back in her apartment, she cleaned out the refrigerator there as her last effort, picked up her suitcase, and left. She'd lived there for almost four years, but she wasn't sorry to be leaving — it was cramped and dark. And there was that one memory she hoped she could put behind her at last.

She had been cruel. There was no way around the truth. She and Alice had slept together several times, and yet when Alice showed up one day unexpectedly Jessica had been completely at a loss about how to act. Spontaneity had never been her strong point.

"I wasn't aware I needed to make an appointment," Alice had said coldly.

11

"I'm very busy. I told you that," she had snapped.

"I see," Alice had said, even more coldly. "Lovers and clients are the same thing."

"My schedule is very tight," Jessica had maintained. "I wish you had called first."

"I doubt I'll call again," Alice had said, walking out the door. "You're wonderful in bed, Jessica, but I don't feel like being squeezed in between appointments."

She had been honest with Alice about being busy. She had made her no-commitments policy clear to Alice, just as she had to everyone since she'd been on her own. But then, Herself recalled, you pursued her. You called her two or three times over two weeks. You rushed her along because it felt good for someone to be there — on *your* terms.

The last she had heard from Alice had been only a few months ago. Alice had joined the People's Temple, a religious cult of some sort. She had cut the conversation short, embarrassed by Alice's pleading with her for money for the Temple's relocation to some South American location. Alice had declared Jessica would repent her sins if she came to just one service.

Sins? Jessica told Herself she had no sins. Her lifestyle was just . . . temporary.

She caught the last possible airport express which would get her to her plane on time and stared out the window. Ever since Alice she'd sworn she'd never get involved with anyone in San Francisco. Affairs would just distract her and make her not want to work so much. It was much, much easier to just call someone she'd met when she got to any particular city. A few hours of pleasure was the only

12

commitment she made and if emotions ran too high there would always be her schedule to take her away again.

As the plane soared eastward, she went through her lecture notes once more, then tried to catch up on her sleep. She shed the past and concentrated on the future, her new home, and her life, which was starting to turn out just as she had planned.

TWO
If It's Chicago, It Must Be . . .

"And I wish each and every one of you the best of luck." Jessica set the marker she had been using as a pointer down in the flip chart tray and graciously nodded as one hundred women in the room applauded enthusiastically.

"You're wonderful," a woman told her a few minutes later. "Do you lecture anywhere else?"

"All over, wherever anyone wants me," Jessica said with a smile.

"Can I have your address?" asked another.

"Here's my card. I'd appreciate a call," Jessica said.

"Excuse me, but I've been wondering if I should wear a suit to the office. Would a suit give me more authority?" a pretty brunette wanted to know as Jessica began to pack up her notes.

"It depends. What do the people on the level above you wear?"

"Suits — pinstripes."

"Then buy yourself a suit, definitely. They'll never promote you if they don't think you'll fit in. You'll have more authority because you'll look like someone with power. If you don't want to be promoted because you like the situation where you are, then wear what everyone else on your level wears."

"I work in a printing office," another woman said, "and a suit is just out of the question. But my subordinates don't take me seriously."

"Hmmm." Jessica frowned. "Think military. Make everything you wear as crisp as you can. Try razor-sharp creases in pants if you wear them. A little thing like that can be the subtle reminder your people need that you are the one in authority. The situation's similar to a police officer who's only wearing trousers and shirt — but there's never any doubt about who's in charge."

"Well, the gun helps," the woman said, laughing.

Laughing easily herself, Jessica answered, "but you can't wear a gun to work, as much as the prospect may appeal to you." She could feel her tension and adrenaline beginning to wear off. "And while you can still act like a human being, remember too much friendliness can result in not being taken seriously when you want something done."

"I'll try it. Thanks for the tip." The woman was smiling gratefully. "You were terrific, really."

"Thank you for coming. Here's my card. Write and let me know how you're doing." She smiled pleasantly and picked up her case.

It had been a long two days, but as always she was the last to leave the seminar room. She stayed as long as any of the women who came to see her wanted to stay. Their personal stories were an endless source of material for her, and they helped her keep current with their concerns and ideas.

Dinner time in Chicago was approaching, but her stomach was still on San Francisco time. She wasn't hungry, just tired. She needed to relax and come down off the high speaking always gave her. It was like acting and it had many of the same rewards. She still remembered her first professional speaking engagement vividly. It was a moment in her life fifteen years ago she could point to and say what went before was Before. Everything After was a different life, a different person.

She had given a short but impassioned speech about the attitudes the business world had toward women. Her fee was twenty dollars, a great amount to the tiny budget of the university women's center. The fee had also been a great amount to her — a symbolic amount. She had begun impartially, describing how women would have to learn the male dominated rules and then work to change them. But the atmosphere of the women's center had been charged with encouragement. She heard someone

16

murmur, "Right on, sister," and felt a fire take hold of her as her voice gained power and conviction.

"They say emotion has no place on the job, that women won't work out because we're emotional. They say showing sympathy for someone in pain is wrong. They say we can't be impartial, that we make up our minds emotionally. But men have demonstrated over and over again that they hire and promote based on emotions, like friendship or trust. When *they* do it they call it gut instinct. When we do it, they sneer and call it woman's intuition.

"Perhaps what they fear is that we won't play the game by their rules. Perhaps we'll use our emotions, our woman's intuition, and make better decisions than they have historically made with their gut instinct. They admit they are afraid, but I don't think they've told the truth about why women frighten them. They're afraid we will succeed." There was applause. "They are afraid we will overcome as we have always overcome." There was another burst of approval. "They are afraid and are not used to fear. They are off-balance. Women must pursue this unique advantage, to survive, to overcome, to succeed, to meet our own needs."

As she left the stage, women touched her, shook her hands, clasped her shoulders, congratulated her.

Her first speaking engagement, and the evening was a triumph. Perhaps that made what happened next easier. Perhaps the exhilaration made her open to new experience, to see returning the fervent embrace of a woman named Phoebe with her own fervor as a simple thing, very easy to do.

Phoebe had asked for nothing. Jessica had asked

for nothing. They each gave freely, passionately, urgently. Phoebe taught thoroughly, Jessica learned quickly, and before the night was over she felt completely reborn. Walking to her own dorm room she marveled at the open ease she had felt giving Jessica to Phoebe for a few hours, sure that afterwards Phoebe would give Jessica back, intact. Never had anything been so easy; never had anything seemed so right.

Relationships with men had always been so hard to work out. After her parents' death she had needed to be self-reliant. Boyfriends came and went. They mostly went after she insisted on keeping a life of her own, and maintaining her business major rather than some course of study men regarded as more "womanly." She'd lost one would-be Romeo when she refused to do less than her best on a test in economics so the other guys wouldn't tease him about dating a brain, and horror of horrors, a libber as well.

Men were too difficult, too demanding. Relationships were never equal, but always lopsided toward the man's needs, the man's power. Ever since that incredible night with Phoebe, she had decided to not seek out men until she was ready to make the major commitment and could take the time to find an equal partner. She would work hard and when she had finally gained her personal goals, she would look around for a more stable relationship with someone who was willing to be as open and free as Phoebe had been.

So she had continued dating women because it was a whole lot easier to get to know a woman than any man she'd ever met. At first she had thought the drifting in her personal life would last just through college. Then just through those first lean years when she'd moved around so much. And then she'd decided she wouldn't worry about men any more at all. Sex was great — when she had sex — but it wasn't the most important aspect of her life.

Jessica kneaded her toes into the hotel room's thinning carpet and sighed. She was dog-tired and couldn't decide how to spend the evening. But she didn't want to sit around remembering the past, wondering about what had happened to Phoebe and Alice and nameless others. Something was very dissatisfying about remembering her past. And if she looked back on her past for too long, something didn't make a lot of sense. Better not to look back at all. Today and tomorrow were all that were important.

Cut the philosophical crap, Herself said, yawning. What are you going to do tonight? She turned down the bed and plumped the pillows, debating about room service. Leaning back, she looked over her airline tickets for the next morning.

Why had she booked such an early flight, she asked Herself. Why do hotels make bedside tables so small? Why do hotels bolt the lamps down so you can't move them out of the way when you're working? Why was she thinking about spending the evening alone when she was in Chicago, Herself wanted to know.

If she were in San Antonio she could call Marilyn. But this wasn't San Antonio, this was Chicago. She fished her address book out of her case. C for Chicago, and Chicago meant Roberta.

"Hello," the soft voice said inquiringly, a little rushed and harried.

"It's Jessica."

"Where are you?" Roberta asked, with wonder and eagerness.

"At O'Hare. I'm filling in for someone. I just found out."

"You must be exhausted."

"I am," Jess said, exhaling heavily. "I am so tired, and I would love to get even more tired." There was a long silence. "Roberta?"

"I'm here, I was just thinking fast. The traffic's awful right now. I couldn't reach you for at least an hour and a half."

"I need a shower and I'll order room service. It'll be waiting when you get here," Jessica murmured. None of the women from the day's lecture would have recognized the low, husky tone. "Champagne, something to nibble on . . ."

"Like you," Roberta suggested.

"I'm hungry too."

"Where are you?"

"Room five-sixty-four at the Marriott. Don't kill yourself getting here."

"I'll try to keep my mind on my driving, but I'm thinking about you, the last time you were here. See you as soon as I can."

Jessica slowly stripped, hanging her suit up carefully. She ordered the champagne and some munchies, then took a quick shower. Toweling her curly black hair, she waited until the food came, signed the bill and then began contemplating Roberta.

If a man had walked up to her the way Roberta had, and asked her right out if she'd like to have a

20

drink, she would have used her eyes to castrate him on the spot. Maybe the skin-tight red satin pants had caught her off guard. Whatever the reason was, she'd said yes, she'd like to have a drink. And later, she'd said yes, she'd like to go to bed.

Roberta had later explained that if she was attracted to a woman she made it plain. She didn't waste any time on women who weren't going to want to go to bed later. She was a consummate pick-up artist and a consummate lover. Jessica hadn't minded being picked up. And right now forgetting about everything and making love for a few hours, no strings, would be wonderful.

A knock on the door brought her out of her fantasizing, remembering the mesh of faces and places and nights. She was breathing hard and was just a little shaky when she opened the door to Roberta.

They hardly exchanged a word. Once the door was closed, Roberta leaned back against it, undoing the tie of her long coat. Jessica took in the black spike heel sandals and the silk stockings. As the coat parted, scarlet garters and a lace garter belt came into view.

The coat slid to the floor. Jessica fell to her knees, kissing the bare abdomen, running her hands over the bare hips, up the firm bare arms, until she brushed the bare breasts. Herself reminded Jessica that Jessica didn't think sex was all that important. Jessica told Herself to mind its own business.

"I didn't want to waste any time undressing," Roberta said and she bent to kiss Jessica's upturned face. Only moments before, her lips had been dry, but now they were wet and hot, pressing feverishly against Roberta's. Roberta broke the kiss and bit urgently at Jessica's lower lip. She became

21

disoriented, feeling drugged and incoherent, lost in passion.

Roberta pressed Jessica down to the floor, and held her body over Jessica. Jessica ran her hands over the firm muscles rippling over Roberta's shoulders, forearms and back. Roberta began brushing over Jessica, flesh touching flesh, hard muscled thighs pressing against Jessica's softer skin.

Roberta taught gymnastics and dance, which gave her endurance. Jessica wallowed in letting Roberta take over completely, submitting gratefully to the other woman's strength. Roberta began working her fingers into Jessica's tired neck muscles, pressing, stroking, pressing, stroking, working her way inch by inch down the length of Jessica's spine. Then the fingers worked their way back up Jessica's shoulder blades. Warm hands caressed her ribs and the soft flesh of the sides of her breasts.

The hands crept to her front, pressing, stroking, then teasing and caressing until she shivered. Roberta drew back, her hands caressing the front of Jessica's body until one finger stroked gently, persistently and the fire burned through Jessica.

She murmured in pleasure, her body arching in response. Rocking, she moved against Roberta who slid both arms around her hips and pressed her mouth into Jessica. Jessica groaned and then sighed deeply.

On and on their lovemaking went, Jessica receiving and giving, swimming and drowning, floating and wading. Her own primal need was frightening and overwhelmed her, and slowly it was filled. She scarcely felt the hardness of the floor under her as on and on the passion consumed her, fingers and tongues

22

and teeth the connection between their straining, needing bodies, meeting in the dark.

As she settled into her seat on the airplane the next morning, she was faintly worried she didn't remember going to bed. She had only the dimmest memory of Roberta leaving after a prolonged and fevered kiss which had almost — but not quite — made Jessica want to pull her back into the bed for the rest of the night. She'd never spent the night with anyone, not the entire night.

She fell asleep almost immediately after take-off, vaguely dreaming about Roberta. They were exhausted dreams of red satin documents with signatures from top to bottom, and rolls of toilet paper dancing on hotel lamps. Her dreams were intruded upon only by the drone of engines and the clink of coffee cups.

THREE
Home Again, Home Again

The place was a royal mess.

Jessica put her suitcase down with a thump and surveyed the stacks of boxes and all her furniture crowded in one corner of the living room. She bent to pick up the key that Vince's Rapid Move had shoved under the door.

With a sigh of depression she went to the kitchen. The movers had even helped themselves to her only cold soda and had used all the ice. She repressed a swell of self-pity, blinked back some tired tears, and wandered into the bedroom.

Well, her bed was in the bedroom. So was the microwave. Jessica smiled while her eyes filled with tears. She felt like Jessica Through the Looking Glass. She went to her office and saw her huge roll-top desk up against the window, all the way across the room from the DESK HERE sign. And the desk was the only furniture that had been put in the office — the books, bookshelves, word processor, and other items all marked OFFICE were in the living room. She tried to decide how much she was going to deduct from what she owed Vince for the botched job. She wondered if Vince would send his Uncle Vito after her if she deducted anything. Maybe she should get Vince to come back and do the job properly.

"It's going to take hours just to be able to sleep tonight," she observed to the empty room. Here you are, in the middle of a mess, Herself said. You were going to pay one way or another, so you should have just gone ahead and paid the penalties. She ignored Herself. She didn't even know where her slacks were, and she had no intention of moving anything while wearing a suit. Shrugging, she had to smile. Her other choice of apparel was the flimsy nightgown in her suitcase, or nothing at all. Moving furniture in the nude was not her idea of a fun time.

"Hel-llo," a voice called from the doorway. Jessica held back a gasp of alarm and then calmed herself. Axe murderers didn't have light, feminine voices. She walked briskly back to the living room remembering she had left the door wide open.

"Excuse me, I hope I didn't startle you."

She had only a brief impression of vaguely

remembered sparkling brown eyes before the envelope in the woman's hand caught her attention. The woman was the one with the grocery bags who she had run into on the doorstep. If she remembered Jessica, she gave no sign.

"The movers asked me to hold onto this for you. They didn't want it to get lost."

Jessica opened the envelope, read the contents, and then laughed mirthlessly. "Of course, the only thing that really mattered to them — the bill. Look at this place," she appealed helplessly.

"Oh dear," the woman sympathized. "It is a mess. I was home, too. If only I'd known, I'd have watched them for you. I'm so sorry." She put her hands on her hips.

Something in the way she stood, even though the woman was several inches shorter than Jessica, made Jessica realize the movers would have done exactly as she asked. "Oh thank you, that's nice of you."

An awkward silence followed and they looked at each other. Jessica smiled. "I'm Jessica Brian."

"Catherine Merrill. Everybody calls me Cat."

"Pleasure to meet you," Jessica said, and they shook hands quite gravely.

Cat raised one shoulder expressively as she surveyed the jumbled mass of furniture and boxes. "They really were thorough. Nothing is where it makes any sense. As I say at work, this is merde."

"The microwave is in the bedroom," Jessica said, and then smiled more naturally as Cat laughed. "And I don't even know how to begin to find something to change into so I can start making sense of this mess."

"I might have something you could fit in," Cat

offered, sizing Jessica up with her eyes. "My jeans would be a couple of inches short, but I'll bet we're the same size."

"No, you're much smaller than me," Jessica protested. Cat was at least four inches shorter, and Jessica was only five-four.

"I'm what you'd call solid pack. Short, but solidly built. Come on, I'll find something. You have to start somewhere." She went across the hall to the other door with Jessica following slowly behind. Jessica realized that even though Cat was shorter, she was plump and generously filled out where Jessica was slender.

Cat was right, they wore the same size. On Cat, the jeans were attractively tight. On her, the jeans hung a little, not clinging at all, and were very short. She looked at her reflection. She didn't own any jeans of her own, just the neatly tailored slacks she'd preferred ever since high school. She looked different somehow, and it wasn't just that the jeans were too short. Maybe it was the different background.

She turned to consider the modern dramatic decor of Cat's bedroom: art nouveau torch lamps, brilliant red comforter on the queen-sized bed, Georgia O'Keeffe print, neat dressing table. The overall effect was very different from her pale blues and traditional oaks.

"A new fashion statement," she announced from the doorway of Cat's bedroom. "But they're a lot better than the nightgown in my suitcase. Thank you very much. I think I'll be able to get the bedroom assembled enough to sleep."

"Let me help you out," Cat volunteered, hopping up. "I'm bored silly."

27

"I really should protest and say I can handle everything myself, but I'm not a fool. You will have to let me buy you dinner at least." She smiled, heartened by Cat's energetic offer.

"Deal."

They went back to Jessica's and surveyed the mess. Fortunately the floors were all hardwood parquet tile. The heavier pieces, including the dressers and bookshelves, slid over the floor with only a little pushing.

Jessica was amazed at Cat's endless energy. Long after she was dying to say, "Enough!" Cat was still sliding boxes and offering to set up the VCR, to plug in the stereo, arrange the records, unpack the stoneware, line the shelves. Jessica was exhausted just watching her.

"Hey, you have all the Chicago albums. They're great, aren't they?" Cat said, sitting down cross-legged in front of the entertainment center, sliding records onto the shelves.

"I was in Boston quite a few years ago and just happened to walk into one of their concerts with a friend. I've been hooked ever since." Boston — Elaine. Elaine was a pleasant memory but she put it aside. She had a policy when she was home to not think about other cities, or the women she made love to in those cities.

"Do you travel a lot?" Cat asked.

"Yes, I'm a consultant and speaker."

"Really? Sounds fascinating."

"It is. I do like to travel, but after a while hotels start looking the same. I have to put the local phone book out where I can see it so I'll remember what city I'm in."

"I know what you mean," Cat said, nodding. "I used to do quite a bit of modeling but all the vanity got pretty tiresome. So I finished up my Bachelor's Degree and now I'm sales manager for the Regency."

"There aren't very many women at that level, are there?" Jessica asked.

"No, I'm one of the first. A lot of women are allowed into sales, especially the pretty ones, but we don't get a chance to show what we can do."

"Do your looks work against you?" Jessica was really curious. She herself wasn't exactly plain, but she wasn't gorgeous, like Cat. Cat's flawless roses and cream complexion didn't come out of a bottle, and neither did her thick golden hair which seemed to style itself no matter how Cat moved.

"Yes," Cat sighed. "The prettier you are, the stupider they think you are. Oh well, I still got the job. And I do still travel, but I spend more time at the hotel than anywhere else, even home."

"Then you should be at home! I knew I shouldn't have let you help me," she protested, guilty about taking so much of apparently scarce free time for Cat.

"Don't be silly. I didn't want to stay home." Jessica saw Cat swallow. "But I'm getting over a relationship that went sour, and all this concentrating on someone else for a while is good therapy. I should be thanking you."

Cat smiled at Jessica, who smiled back. "And I'm so glad I got to know you, too," she went on. "I've lived in this building for two years, and I was still only on nodding terms with the couple that used to live here. It's hard to break the ice, especially when I don't work a regular nine-to-five job."

"I know what you mean." Jessica sat down on the

29

floor alongside Cat, to help put the records away. There were nearly six hundred of them and Jessica had them strictly organized lest her coveted Christopher Parkening Bach get too close to her coveted The Beverly Hillbillies Sing, the first album she'd ever bought. They worked in companionable silence for awhile, then Cat asked if she could put on one of the albums.

"Sure. I want to knock off, anyway. I think I'm going to have to welch on the dinner offer, at least until after I get some sleep."

"Now I'm the one who's been thoughtless. Where are you back from?"

"Chicago."

"Wretched plane trip, too, I'll bet. I always hated that run. It's so boring and usually not in a bigger jet, either."

"Yeah, a Seven-thirty-seven, packed." Jessica lay back on the floor, not minding the hardness, and sighed with a mixture of tiredness and satisfaction. Though far from finished, her new home was almost bearable. "I haven't heard this album in longer than I want to remember," she said, beginning to hum "Baby I'm-a Want You."

"I wish I could say the same," Cat whispered, and she got up off the floor without the bounce and energy she'd had for the last few hours.

"Shall I turn it off?" Jessica asked.

"Please," Cat said, walking to the window. "I was stupid to put it on. I thought I could handle the memories."

"I'm sorry."

"Don't be. It was 'our' song and I was hoping it

30

wouldn't bother me." She turned back to Jessica, her soft eyes bright with tears. "Why are the bastards so hard to get over? Paul was such a jerk, but sometimes I miss him."

"Do you miss him, or just being with someone?" Jessica asked philosophically. Paul . . . well, she wouldn't have believed for a minute Cat wasn't straight, so it was really no surprise.

"Oh, I tell myself I'm just lonely, but I miss the way he shaved in the morning, you know, little stuff like that."

Jessica didn't know. She'd never had the time to live with anyone, but if she told Cat that, Cat would think she was some kind of prude. She didn't want to alienate her neighbor. Besides, knowing someone in the building would mean her plants wouldn't die when she was out of town. She thought for a moment, then said, "Changes are hard on the body and soul, but I've always believed when a door closes, another opens." Herself begged Jessica not to burst into song — particularly not "Look to the Rainbow" or "Climb Every Mountain." I'm just sensible, she told Herself. What about the little black book, Herself asked, smirking. Shut up, she told Herself.

"What kind of consultant are you?" Cat asked, summoning up a smile.

"Assertiveness, self-image, particularly for women in management positions. I got into it early, and now I'm an old-timer in the field."

"You? An old-timer?"

"I hardly believe it myself. I'm thirty-four, but five years ago assertiveness was a new field. And there were only a few women in management positions. Now there are more women and the field keeps growing. I was in the right place at the right time."

"So how's my self-image?" Cat asked, laughing as she wiped dust off her nose and smoothed her tousled blonde hair.

"For a volunteer mover, you are pure executive material."

"Thanks. My ego needs all the boosting it can get."

"Any time," Jessica said, then yawned before she could stop.

"I'm going, you don't have to be rude." Cat grinned and grabbed her keys.

Suddenly Jessica couldn't keep her eyes open any longer. She locked the door behind Cat and tumbled into bed.

FOUR
Awakenings

Fortune smiled on Jessica. All the work, all the waiting, all the persistent following up on consulting and speaking leads paid off all at once.

A new computer software company gave her carte blanche to design and implement an overall in-service training program for sales personnel: presentation styles, client relations, clothing, the works. The experience was a heady one. Likening it to playing

God, Jessica spent a lot of time with the salespeople and less time on the road.

She conducted two one-day workshops, one in Los Angeles and one in San Jose, each paying handsome fees. Repeat sessions were being scheduled for Sacramento and San Diego.

The sun came out and stayed out for almost two weeks, a very unusual event for the San Francisco spring. She took the good weather as an omen for her positive future.

She was completely absorbed in her work, as she had been for the last ten years. Each day she watered her plants and did just enough housework to keep her place looking as it had when she moved in. Falling asleep at night she reminded herself that life had never been better, that everything she had worked for was finally paying off, and that in a month or so she would be heading for San Antonio, and she would see Marilyn again.

Marilyn was special. Meeting her, Jessica had been a bee drawn to sweet southern honey. The women in her little black book were just bed partners, except Marilyn. They talked on the phone often to keep up on each other's life. If there was anyone she wanted to spend more time with, it was Marilyn. As president of The Place Corporation, Marilyn had become a role model for Jessica's classes, a stellar example of a woman succeeding on her own terms.

"I can hardly wait, love," Marilyn said when Jessica called to confirm when she would be arriving. "I'm really looking forward to seeing you again. I knew you'd be back, but it has been a long time."

"I'm excited too, in more ways than one, if you

34

know what I mean," she said, the smile in her voice carrying across the line to Marilyn.

"Minx."

"Did you know nobody talks like you?"

"Like what?"

"I know lots of southern belles, and none of them calls anyone else a minx. I think you cultivate that accent."

"Now whay would Ah do that?" Marilyn asked innocently.

Jessica could hear the Scarlett O'Hara coming out. "So people will think you're stupid. Then they underestimate you. Then you walk away with all the winnings."

"Really, Jess, Ah don't know where you get such ideas," Marilyn protested.

Jessica giggled. Even over long distance, she could picture Marilyn batting her eyelashes.

"You got the plans for your hotel past the city's no-growth stance, didn't you? In front of several chains with expensive lawyers."

"Well, I guess I must have made them an offer they couldn't refuse."

"Um-hmmm. I'll just bet."

"What does that mean?" Marilyn's voice was suddenly a lot cooler, a lot less honeyed.

"I was just teasing," Jessica protested.

"I certainly hope so. I didn't put out to get my development plan approved."

"I'm sorry, I didn't mean to imply you did. I just meant you have considerable charm, of which I'm only too aware."

"Hmph. I offered the City Council something no

35

one else could. The Place brings the city a new reputation, a convention area that's safe and appealing to women — not just businesswomen, but the wives of all those businessmen who come to San Antonio, too. We have the highest volume food service for walk-in business on the Riverwalk."

"Okay, okay, I'm convinced you're special," she said with a laugh. "I didn't mean to impugn the honor of your establishment."

"We are unique." Marilyn's voice grew warmer again. "Like you're unique."

"How am I unique?"

"You know the answers to people's questions."

"Is that why you bought me a drink after my session ended? To answer questions?"

"Well, the way you're shaped had something to do with my interest. I find it hard to keep — What?" Marilyn's voice faded as she spoke to someone else in the room. "Yes, I'll talk to him. Jess, honey, I have to go. I've been trying to reach this fella all week. I think he may be able to put me in touch with the capital I need to expand."

"How exciting! If you get any definite word, call me, I'd love to hear about your plans."

"You'll be almost the first to know. Bye-bye."

She leaned back in her desk chair. Marilyn was energetic and insightful, and Jessica had been stunned when a few drinks and a generally serious discussion about business had ended with them in bed. But there was more than sex between them. Today she had been feeling an urge to share what was happening in her life, and she had wanted to spend the entire afternoon talking to Marilyn, and hear about someone else's life.

At sunset she turned off the word processor and went to sit in the living room. From her window she could see the sun setting behind the building-covered hills. On impulse she put on Chuck Mangione's "Feels So Good." She pulled her knees up to her chin and rocked slowly, noting Venus as it emerged in the darkening sky.

What next, Herself wanted to know. She told Herself to go away. What next, Herself persisted. I don't know, she answered. I don't know what comes next. I worked so long, so single-mindedly to be at peace, to have this place, to be free from immediate financial worries. I don't know what comes next.

Herself wasn't satisfied with not knowing and promptly tormented her with memories: how much fun it had been to go out with Alice, how good it was to talk to Marilyn, how wonderful life might be if Marilyn and Alice and Roberta and all the other women were always at her fingertips, each being exactly what she needed, when she needed, without demanding anything in return.

Dream on, she told Herself. That's the most idiotic, unrealistic, selfish reality a person could have, she told Herself. Herself laughed and muttered something about Jessica not having looked in a mirror lately. She shut off the music, turned on all the lights and watched M*A*S*H. Herself decided not to compete with the TV. Jessica was very glad.

She heard the door across the hall close and remembered she owed Cat dinner. Fresh air would be good for her. She hustled across the hall and knocked on Cat's door.

"Hi, I owe you dinner, remember? I know it's late, but how about tonight?"

"I was just thinking I couldn't stand another frozen dinner." Cat grinned, and pushed her curls back away from her face with a tired gesture. "Been on my feet all day. A fire fighters' convention. They started two fires and two fights and several groups were beginning elevator races just as I left."

"Why don't you change and then tell me what elevator races are over dinner," Jessica said.

She felt a hell of a lot better. She went home again and found her credit cards. Soon there was a bang on the door.

"I hope we're not going any place fancy," Cat announced. She had changed into a well-washed pair of blue jeans and a big shirt. Cat looked fashionable and comfortable and Jessica felt a surge of envy. She hadn't felt comfortable for a week now.

"I don't know if it's fancy or not. You pick the place. Sky's the limit." Jessica indicated her own neatly pressed slacks and walking shoes. "I'm not dressed for haute cuisine either, though."

"There's a terrific, and I mean terrific, Italian place not too far away. We can walk. We'll need the walk coming back to keep from being sick from stuffing ourselves in an undignified fashion."

"That good? I love Italian food."

"Especially garlic bread."

"White sauces," Jessica said as she locked her door and they walked down the hall. "I'll even eat liver with a white sauce on it."

"Ravioli, so fresh the spinach in the filling isn't completely limp."

"There's this place in Chicago with the most spectacular rigatoni —"

"Ricci's!" Cat exclaimed. They walked up a couple of blocks, each describing in complete detail their most orgiastic Italian food experiences. By the time they got to the restaurant, Jessica was starving too.

"A large basket of garlic bread," Cat ordered when the waitress came over.

"And a bottle of wine. What's the house label?" Jessica discussed the wine briefly with the waitress.

"You know wines?" Cat asked, sipping her water.

"A little. I've been collecting some reds and whites for a few years now. It's just a hobby."

"My taste is very unlearned," Cat admitted freely. "Isn't rosé a mix of white and red?"

Jessica tried to keep her face expressionless. "No, actually, it's not," she said seriously. Cat burst out laughing and Jessica realized she was being teased. Where was her sense of humor?

"You should have seen your face," Cat said. "It was as if you were saying to yourself, Is this woman an idiot? and trying not to show it."

Jessica smiled. "You really had me going —" She broke off as the waitress delivered the garlic bread. It was at least a half a loaf, pungently grilled with garlic butter and liberally sprinkled with fresh Parmesan cheese and chili powder.

"Isn't San Francisco a wonderful place?" Cat asked with her mouth full of bread. "The best of everything."

"That's why I chose to live here. The weather in New York is terrible most of the time and the atmosphere is too hard."

"I know what you mean. I lived in New York for exactly three months. I understand why New Yorkers love it. But I was raised in California, so I really found it hard to adapt. So I came back. Politics are better here, too."

"I agree with you," Jessica said earnestly. Usually she avoided talking politics with acquaintances, but something told her she and Cat wouldn't disagree. "I can't say I care much for Jerry Brown as a person, but he has tried to make California more liberal."

"I meant San Francisco politics, actually. I like the Board of Supervisors being elected from local districts. Hey, I read they're going to overhaul the Cable Cars," Cat volunteered. "I don't know how it might affect tourism income, but apparently they'll be shut down for over two years."

"Does the Regency rely a lot on tourists?"

"Not people off the street. We can handle convention tourists, like the damn firefighters. Oh yeah, elevator races are where two people get on at the same floor and then they race to see who can get to the top floor, chug-a-lug a beer and get back to the starting floor again first. If it's the convention championship at stake, it can take all night."

"But what about the people trying to use the elevators?" Jessica asked. She'd never heard of elevator races. Maybe her childhood was just too sheltered, she told Herself.

"That's the element of chance, I guess. Did I mention that they started two fires?"

"Yes. How?"

"Apparently they were trying to see how long it would take someone else to spot it. They put the fires out, very efficiently. We only lost two tablecloths and singed one small piece of carpeting." Cat grimaced. "The problem with most conventions is they're mostly male. You cannot believe the games men alone can get up to."

"I think I can imagine." She knew she wouldn't last a day in Cat's job. She couldn't handle it when people were childish. She had been an adult all her life, the result of having elderly parents. Everything she did in her life was rational.

Keeping a woman in every port for example, Herself said snidely.

Certainly. Sex is in the proper perspective, she informed Herself firmly. Herself just laughed and laughed.

She and Cat chatted on about a variety of topics and only disagreed on one.

"But how can you judge a movie you haven't seen?" Cat persisted.

"I don't have to see a movie to know what it's about," Jessica said.

"Yes you do. How else do you experience popular culture? I'll warn you now, I studied popular culture in college. I *was* popular culture in college. I have definite prejudices," Cat emphasized, her eyes dancing. "I prefer things made in this century, so I love movies and rock 'n' roll and Andy Warhol. Not necessarily in that order."

Jessica laughed and agreed to go to the movies on the weekend. Despite Cat's modern tastes, Jessica decided she was a very interesting person. I would be better off to take a little more interest in the world around me and rely a little less on books, she said to Herself.

"I'm dying," Jessica told Cat as they began the walk home.

"We could lie down and just roll home," Cat

41

suggested. "Wait!" Cat held her breath for a moment, then burped. She grinned. "Excuse me, but that felt wonderful. I feel much better now." God, Jessica thought, she's so free.

"I need some Seven-Up. That always makes me burp," she said after a moment. Had she ever been as young as Cat seemed, as free?

"I have some. Why do we do this to ourselves?"

"Freud would say we have destructive impulses."

"Screw Freud. I think we're just pigs."

"That describes us very aptly," Jessica agreed, then she smiled. "Did you see the look on the waitress's face when we ordered more garlic bread?"

Cat burst out laughing. "Don't make me laugh, Jessica, it hurts," she gasped, holding one side.

Jessica laughed as Cat clung to a telephone pole. "They're probably erecting a plaque to us, memorializing our table."

"Oh, stop. I can't walk if I'm laughing," Cat said, pushing away from the pole.

They staggered the rest of the way, laughing about dinner and laughing at the looks they were getting from other people. They probably think we're a couple of crazy women, Jessica told Herself when they got in the elevator. Herself observed that this being San Francisco, people probably thought they were a pair of dykes.

She felt a sudden chill take over her, and she stole a sideways glance at Cat. Her heart began to pound so loudly she couldn't hear anything else. What are you saying, she demanded of Herself. We're just friends. Would people think we're lovers? Cat isn't a lesbian, she's straight. And I'm not a lesbian either, she told Herself. Life has just been easier with women, that's all. Herself laughed unpleasantly and she shivered.

They each had a glass of Seven-Up, and Cat applauded when Jessica finally burped and felt better.

"I have some ice cream at my place," Jessica offered, her voice a little strained. She wondered if she were pale.

"Are you kidding? I couldn't eat anything for at least a week," Cat said. "I want to go to bed."

Jessica choked in mid-swallow. She gasped for breath and coughed violently, tears streaming from her eyes. Cat thumped her on the back until Jessica signaled that she wasn't choking to death. Cat couldn't possibly be suggesting — no, she couldn't. Jessica was beset by fears, wondering if Cat was bisexual, wondering if Cat was going to make a pass at her. Wondering why she was so damn afraid of Cat suddenly, and so afraid to go home and be alone with Herself.

Cat lay down on her sofa, one hand on her stomach, groaning. "Thanks for dinner, Jessica. Really. I may die from it, but thanks for a great last meal."

"You're welcome," Jessica managed, and suddenly they were talking again as they had at the restaurant.

Much later, she looked at the stars again. They were sparkling down at a very different person, she felt. Who was she? Was she really a lesbian? Had she been kidding Herself all these years, making excuses for her real sexual preference, with patent lies such as not having enough time to develop a relationship with a man?

Herself said yes, you are a lesbian. Yes, you've

43

been fooling yourself. And you've done a first-class job of it, too.

What if people found out, the people who brought her contracts? What if they found out she'd only slept with women? Did everyone know Jessica Brian was a lesbian, everyone but Jessica?

* * * * *

The panicky feeling stayed with her. For days when Jessica met with clients she read double meanings into people's words, imagined they were slyly suggesting something. At night she lay in a ball on her bed, wondering, agonizing.

How could she have practiced self-deception so thoroughly? Why had she taken so long to see the obvious truth? She hadn't made some rational, logical choice to be with women, no matter how much she wanted to pretend. She was a lesbian. She *wanted* to be with women, for physical and emotional reasons. Logic had little to do with it.

On a foggy afternoon a week later she was closing a consultation with one of the sales reps at the software company.

"You're really quite special," the woman said, shaking Jessica's hand. When she didn't immediately let go, Jessica pulled her hand away, her heart pounding, her color rising.

"Thank you," she said brusquely. "I try."

The woman's face fell a little, but she smiled at Jessica again. "The day's over for you, isn't it? Would you like to go have a drink?"

"No. No thanks, really. I do have another appointment this evening, and just enough time to make it home to change to a fresh suit." The suit she was wearing wasn't crumpled, and it was a weak excuse.

"Another time, perhaps, then."

When the woman left, Jessica looked down at her shaking hands. "What's happening to me?" she whispered.

She packed up hurriedly and half-ran to the bus. She ran to her building and up the stairs, locking her door behind her. Her heart was pounding. She sat down on the sofa, her head in her hands.

Herself tried to reason with her. That woman was just being friendly, admiring you because you're professionally admirable. She wasn't making a pass, just an overture of friendship. And you acted as if you thought she was going to attack you. You wanted to ask her why she thought you were gay. You wanted to demand who she thought she was that she could assume you were available. You're losing your mind, Jessica, losing your mind.

She got up and rummaged around until she came up with a bottle of scotch. She hated scotch but started drinking anyway.

You went with Roberta that first night because you wanted to. Your body wanted hers.

No! She tried to reassemble the shreds of the argument she'd been using for years to excuse her preference for women. I went with Roberta because I chose to. Because I could have just as easily said no. Because it was safer, less risky than going with a man. I just never had the motivation to try it with a man, that's all.

Liar! Herself lost patience with Jessica. You like women, you've always preferred women to men.

45

You're afraid of being tagged gay, that's all. You'll advise women in your classes to go out and conquer, be honest and be themselves. But not you, not for yourself.

She had another shot of scotch. You make me sound like a hypocrite, she told Herself.

You are. Got to hand it to you, when you do something you do it well. You don't have the courage of your convictions. You don't let anyone stay the whole night with you, not because they might think your relationship is something it isn't, but because it might prove to *you* that you're a lesbian.

No! That can't be why.

She had another shot, then another. Not used to hard liquor, she broke out in a sweat.

What did you do when that asshole in college started feeling you up at the student pub?

I slugged him. I would have slugged a woman who started copping a feel without my permission.

He bought you a drink.

That didn't give him rights.

Roberta bought you a drink. You went to bed with her.

That was different . . .

How?

She was . . .

Yes?

. . . a woman.

She drank another shot down. It came right back up. Herself left her in peace while she threw up and then slowly, miserably, undressed. Sweating profusely, she crawled into bed.

Are you a lesbian, or not, Herself asked slyly.

I don't know.

What's a lesbian, Herself asked quietly.

I don't know. She rides a motorcycle, I guess. She's alone.

What a stereotype. Like Marilyn, Herself pointed out.

Marilyn. Marilyn wasn't alone, she wasn't obsessed with sex, she didn't own a motorcycle and she was a respected businesswoman. And she was a lesbian. She had told Jessica so, quite firmly.

And Jessica had been shocked. Lying in bed with the smell of Marilyn on her, the feel of Marilyn's hair against her breasts, she had been shocked to think she was in bed with a lesbian. And she'd driven the reality of her own sexual preference successfully out of her mind.

I'm afraid, she told Herself.

I don't blame you. Lots of women are afraid. Don't you teach that in your courses? Teacher teach thyself, Herself suggested.

I tell women to make their image and then stay with it, to take the consequences and the rewards together. I've been hiding this big piece of myself. I was showing the world only a part of me, and showing myself the exact same face.

How does this change things, Herself asked.

She sat up but decided that sitting up was a major mistake. She carefully laid her throbbing head back on the pillows. I feel different. I feel scared. I feel alone.

* * * * *

She finished up a proposal for an in-service

47

training seminar for a large San Francisco bank. She sealed the envelope and sat back.

She'd been hiding in her room for days now, almost afraid to even look in the mirror. She was afraid DYKE would be written across her forehead. Herself told her she was being ridiculous.

Just give me a little time, she pleaded. I'll get used to this. The knock at the door shattered the oppressive silence surrounding her.

Cat stormed in. She hardly paused for breath. "Do you have any cold wine? Beer? I can't believe my boss is such a bastard. The waiters are on strike and there weren't any strawberries. Can you believe how muggy it is? I wish there was some sunshine. What a merde of a day." She went through the living room like a whirlwind, then into the kitchen where she grabbed a can of coke out of the refrigerator, then left it on the coffee table.

She dropped into the rocker and rocked furiously. "I'm not tough enough with the conference planners. The damned union won't give up even one thing to get enough people on the floor to meet the obligations for tomorrow's events. I can't get any contracts signed until the strike clears up, and he says I'm not tough enough with the conference planners!"

You're not making a lot of sense, Cat," Jessica observed.

"Do I have to make sense with you?" she asked plaintively. "I've been coherent and logical all day long. I just want to gripe for a while."

"Okay with me. What should I do?"

"Say poor Cat and how awful."

"Okay. Poor Cat."

48

Cat glanced at Jessica, grinned, and rocked furiously. "Two of the sales reps are having an affair and I think they're padding their expense accounts and traveling on our money to sleep together since they're both married. So another thirty-five cents an hour is going to cure all of the union's problems. I just don't know."

"How awful." Jessica was relieved Cat hadn't noticed anything different about her. Maybe to Cat she wasn't any different.

"Let's go get drunk at O'Malley's."

Jessica hesitated. She felt very fragile and somehow completely overwhelmed by Cat's energy. Forgetting all about everything sounded quite tempting. She still remembered the scotch hangover and promised Herself moderation. "Okay. Just a little tipsy."

O'Malley's was a simple neighborhood bar just down the block and around the corner. It was a little early for the usual crowd, Cat explained, and she and Jessica slid into the recesses of a booth with two Long Island iced teas.

"This stuff ought to do the trick," Jessica said after a taste. The drink was very strong, but it went down very easy.

"Mmm. It's made of one-part of just about everything that's over a hundred and twenty proof with a dash of Coke for color." Cat took a big sip. "Merde, what a day."

"So I gathered," Jessica said. "Are you French?"

"No, why?"

"Merde."

"Oh," Cat said, and she smiled slightly. "My dad would beat the merde out of me if I swore. My gym teacher was French and I picked up her favorite swear word. My dad never knew what it meant."

"Where's your dad now?" Jessica asked.

"He and my mom died," Cat closed her eyes for a second as if to concentrate, "four and a half years ago. Continental pair that they were, they were speeding down the autobahn when they went into a skid."

"I'm sorry," Jessica said.

"They were together," Cat said, and she shrugged, but Jessica sensed that under the nonchalance Cat had adored her parents.

"Well, you can go ahead and complain. You don't have to make any sense, but I'm listening."

"That's nice to know," Cat said with a sigh. She leaned back in the booth and closed her eyes. "I really don't need to talk. Today was just one of those days. I talked to myself the whole way home. One thing after another kept coming to mind that I wanted to bitch about. It's good just to know there's someone to listen."

Jessica leaned back too, glad she wasn't sitting in her place agonizing. If she drank enough Long Island iced tea, maybe she could forget about all the suddenly unanswerable questions. Damn the hangover. Marilyn had said that Jessica always knew the answers. What a laugh!

Cat was rambling on about nothing in particular, and Jessica remembered to say Poor Cat and How awful occasionally. It was nice and undemanding.

She looked around the bar and noticed how many couples there were. In another booth opposite, across the bar, two women were huddled close together, laughing softly as they clinked glasses. They were oblivious to anyone who might be staring at them, including Jessica. She glanced around. She *was* the only one staring at them. But they made such a lovely picture. She wanted to remember the contented, beautiful faces, the light from the sputtering candle illuminating the lovers with a benevolent glow.

"You look kind of strange, Jessica," Cat observed, and Jessica came back to reality with a bump.

"I do?"

"Yes. As if you had bad news."

"No, nothing like that. Just trying to make a decision."

"What kind of decision?"

"Between two choices, and I can't have both, just one or the other."

"Hmmm. I hate those kind of choices. There's usually no going back."

"Bingo. Ford at the road, so to speak." She was surprised she could speak so lightly about something that was beginning to gnaw at her insides. She felt as if she were going to explode. Who am I? What am I? What am I going to do?

Are you really any different, Herself wanted to know.

I don't know.

"Earth to Jessica."

"Sorry. This is powerful elixir," she said, waving a hand at her drink.

"Guaranteed amnesia. Forget your troubles. Have another."

"No, I'm pleasantly fuzzy at the moment. Let's go get some pizza around the corner." The picture the two women made was beginning to look so tempting that she wanted to go over and ask them how they'd

51

achieved such beauty between them. She needed to leave before she completely lost her sense of propriety. Screw propriety, Herself said.

They found they both hated anchovies. They quickly disposed of a medium pepperoni and a pitcher of icy beer. Sated, they wandered back home again.

"Why did I eat in my suit?" Cat asked.

"Because you were all worked up and wanted to go out."

"We could have put on some jeans."

"I don't own any," Jessica admitted, rather ashamedly.

"What!" Cat exclaimed shrilly. "No jeans? What do you do when you want to relax?"

"I wear slacks, a sweater. What I'm wearing now."

"With make-up and nylons? Girl, don't you know how to relax? Don't you have any T-shirts?"

"Where would I wear them to?"

"Nowhere, silly," Cat lectured. "You put on a T-shirt and some jeans and you lay around. You don't have to impress anyone. My favorite T-shirt says 'Live long and prosper' on it."

"Guess I need to buy some jeans," Jessica ventured as the elevator stopped at the third floor and the cage doors slid slowly open.

" 'Night," Cat said. "Hey, wait a minute." Jessica hesitated, her key in the lock while Cat disappeared. After a few moments and some frantic rustlings, Cat reappeared. "Here. You gotta start somewhere."

She took the bundle and mumbled a thank you. As she undressed and hung up her slacks in the "cleaners" part of the closet, she remembered the bundle she'd put down with her purse and padded back to the living room for it.

Holding it up in the bedroom, she had to laugh. It was a worn purple T-shirt that said WOMEN DO IT BETTER & LOOK BETTER DOING IT. It smelled of laundry softener and Cat's subtle perfume.

She held it against her body for a moment, then put it on and went to sleep.

* * * * *

"Hi, neighbor! Hang on a second," she called, and she ran up the steps to take one of the grocery bags from Cat.

"Thanks, you saved my life! That's the one with the eggs, of course, and it was going to fall any second."

"Why do you always try to bring the groceries up in one trip?" Jessica asked as she unlocked the door to the building and rang for the elevator.

"Because I do. Don't know why. It's a compulsion, I guess. Could you get my door?" Cat asked breathlessly as they got out on the third floor.

Jessica carried the bag into the small kitchen. Cat set her bags down with a thump and gave a satisfied sigh. She asked, "Would you like a diet Pepsi? Or how about a glass of wine? It's Friday and I'm actually off for three whole days in a row."

"What kind of wine?" Jessica asked. "I'm very picky." She realized rather suddenly that she felt comfortable with Cat.

"It's ordinary Chablis, miz conniesewer." Cat pulled the cork out of a half-finished bottle and poured them both a glass, then went back to unpacking the groceries.

Jessica sipped in peace, noticing how graceful Cat was, how her hair shone in the dim kitchen light.

Look, Herself said, I wanted you to realize you were a lesbian. But that doesn't give you license to start mooning over every woman you see. You'd be as bad as some construction worker then.

But I'm not mooning, just admiring. Cat's straight. I'm not in any danger of getting involved. Herself muttered.

"I was thinking of making lasagna for dinner. Would you like some?"

"Home-cooked food? Really?" Jessica almost squealed. "I didn't know anyone cooked any more."

"I do when I have the time. Lasagna's easy. I'll show you as I go."

"Don't bother. I'm all thumbs in the kitchen. Teaching me is pointless."

"How do you survive?"

"I eat out and pray several times daily to my miraculous microwave. It's the only thing between me and starvation." Cat giggled and Jessica grinned, too. "By the way, I'm off to San Antonio tomorrow, I'll be back in about four days. Would you water my plants on Wednesday?"

"Sure, convention or seminar?"

"Convention. I would be loyal and stay at the Regency —"

"It's gorgeous in San Antonio, opens right onto the Riverwalk —"

"— but everything's at The Place."

"What's that?" Cat asked, her nose wrinkling.

Jessica knew Cat tended to disapprove of hotels

she hadn't heard of, so she explained. "A hotel owned and managed mostly by women. It's for traveling businesswomen — the entire concept is. The restaurant has mostly single and double tables. The bar is more like a reading room with a waitress. I know the owner and she's been getting good signals to raise the capital to expand to New York."

"Sounds interesting. I've been on the GM's — the general manager's — case to restructure the tenth story lounge to accommodate more singles escaping from their rooms for a few hours."

"Same idea. Part of The Place is also available for lease — corporate living quarters."

"Sounds nice. Do you think," Cat said impulsively, "I mean, would you mind if sometime I arranged one of my inspection tours to coincide with one of your speaking trips? I like to sightsee but I hate doing it on my own."

"Sure," Jessica said, having hesitated for a split second. "I have a trip to New York in October, the best time of year."

"That gives me a couple of months to see if I can come up with a good excuse for a trip. Let's compare calendars later and make some plans. I'm excited already."

The wine was actually quite acceptable, Jessica decided after her second glass. Cat had convinced her to have a go at layering the lasagna. To Jessica's surprise, the dish came out fine. Maybe the credit was owed to Cat's teaching technique. Maybe it was the way she had guided Jessica's hands with her own, standing next to her while she worked. Maybe it was the fact that Cat didn't care if the process was messy — she just laughed.

"Don't sweat it, Jessica. There are more important things like how the lasagna tastes."

"You're right, taste is more important than looks." Herself shrieked and Jessica fought a blush.

Cat said, "I know a place called Gallager's where the prime rib is not only wonderful, but the servings are huge, worth every penny." Cat grinned and began describing other places she'd like to see when they went to New York.

Jessica relaxed and told Herself not to read double entendres into everything she said. I can be comfortable with Cat . . . I don't have to watch my words, she thought. Herself gave a defeated moan.

Later, tossing and turning, Jessica wondered if she'd made a mistake. She and Cat would probably get on quite well, and have a great time in New York when they weren't working. But after the way she'd stared at Cat tonight, she wondered if she was in danger of having too good a time.

She yanked her thoughts away from Cat, Cat's eyes, Cat's hair, Cat's smile, Cat's laugh, Cat's cooking, Cat's swearing, Cat's walk. San Antonio, think about San Antonio, she told Herself.

San Antonio and Marilyn. Marilyn who called once a week just to talk and give and ask advice. Marilyn, who more than any of the others, was the closest thing to a lover she had. Marilyn, who would help Jessica sort out her mixed up feelings.

FIVE
Two and Fro

A long black limousine with *The Place* discreetly written on the door was waiting for Jessica. The ride from the airport into the Riverwalk district was long, and in July the weather was unbearably sticky.

The airline had oversold first class, and she had grudgingly accepted coach in return for a free upgrade to first class next time she flew. Her seat had ended up being directly in front of a five-year old whose quiet absorption in the airplane's mystery ended precisely three minutes after take-off. By the time the plane reached San Antonio, she didn't think the free upgrade had been nearly adequate compensation. But the limo was wonderfully cool, the ride refreshingly smooth, and she began to feel that she might be able to separate her blouse from her body without major surgery.

She had worn her most comfortable clothes, knowing that San Antonio would be claustrophobic, but even so, her cool cotton slacks and blouse were now a second skin. She wished she had just worn jeans and a T-shirt as Cat had suggested. She now owned a pair of jeans, but the subject of her own self-image was very fragile at the moment. She wasn't any more ready to travel in jeans than she was to admit openly she was a lesbian.

She tried to look poised and calm when she reached the hotel. She found, gratefully, that Marilyn had seen to it she was already checked in and would be taken directly to her suite without waiting.

The bellman set her bags out, explained the room's amenities, introduced her to the authentic English butler, and then refused his tip, explaining that Ms. Spartla would have his hide if he accepted it.

"As Ms. Spartla's guest, Madam, everything is on the house," the butler explained, and he left Jessica gazing around her in awe.

She had stayed at The Place twice before and had thought the regular guest rooms quite an experience. They didn't bolt the lamps to the tables. But this suite was . . . decadent. There was no other word for it. The suite was two-storied, with a striking fifteenth floor view of the sprawling San Antonio area. The carpet was deep and soft enough to sleep on.

On her last trip, on the last night, she had met Marilyn. They had shared a wonderful evening of wine and lovemaking. When they weren't making love they were talking about their careers, sharing professional advice and telling stories. And Marilyn had assured her the next time Jessica came to San Antonio she'd find out just how they did things in Texas. She hadn't been prepared for quite this much hospitality. Repaying it would be a challenge and quite probably, recalling Marilyn's passionate nature, very enjoyable.

She spent fifteen minutes exploring the suite. The bathroom alone was a religious experience. This, she told Herself, is quite possibly the most hedonistic arrangement I've ever seen. Herself urged her to take advantage of the opportunity, so she started water running from the four taps which filled the huge sunken tub. It was larger than most jacuzzis and she was looking forward to a long cool soak before going over her notes for tomorrow's lecture.

The doorbell rang and she went to answer it, feeling absolutely adolescent in her delight over having a doorbell to her hotel room. A waiter wheeled in a cart, set out several items expertly and quickly, bowed, and vanished.

There was a large bowl of strawberries, another of peaches, fresh cream, an assortment of crackers and cheese, and two snifters of brandy, resting in holders over a low flame. She salivated and then shivered with anticipation. Marilyn did everything thoroughly, took her time, and was only satisfied with the best.

The doorbell rang again and this time Marilyn was there. She greeted Jessica in her cool way, and went to the phone. Jessica watched her, slowly appraising the long legs, and the perfect body which was only partially disguised under an exquisite black suit. It would be impossible for anyone to forget Marilyn was a woman, but Jessica had seen Marilyn's style at work — she countered the warmth of her beauty with an extreme coolness of attitude that stopped flirtation cold. Yet Jessica was willing to bet Marilyn's employees believed she was competent and fair.

At the moment, however, Jessica wasn't concerned with Marilyn's competence. She imagined the buttons of Marilyn's blouse slowly coming undone. Jessica felt her body flush with desire and carefully examined her feelings. The last time with Marilyn she would have said the breathless passion she felt was just a natural and understandable desire for sex. Now she admitted the truth. She wanted to be with a woman. She wanted to feel soft skin and taste Marilyn's passion because Marilyn was a woman.

The truth at last, Herself crowed. See, it wasn't that hard.

I'm shaking like a leaf inside, scared to death, and you think it wasn't hard to admit? She snapped out of her reverie when she realized Marilyn was watching her with her cool intimate smile as she spoke into the phone.

"I'm in fifteen hundred, but you can call only if there's a fire, and then only if it's on this floor. Otherwise you handle it. Thanks, Suzanne. Hello, James, this is Marilyn. I'm in fifteen hundred and Ms. Brian and I would like complete privacy until further notice. Thank you." Her voice had a soft drawl, but she gave instructions with a poise commanding assent and respect.

"I can finally relax, Jessie," Marilyn said as she turned from the phone. "You look washed out, darlin'," she added, the drawl coming out fully, the tone changing from professional to personal. "Let me help you relax."

"I was going to take a bath," Jessica said. "I don't feel very relaxed at the moment. And thank you for all this. I'm a little overwhelmed."

"I worked hard for this place and it gives me incredible pleasure to share it with someone I care about and who appreciates it," Marilyn said, walking toward Jessica. She put her hands on Jessica's shoulders. "We're also lucky there weren't any Presidents in town, or we'd have been in the Junior Suite. The bathtub is much smaller in the Junior Suite." She pressed her cool lips against Jessica's for a moment. Jessica's pulses leapt with the thrill of it. Her body responded to Marilyn. "The bathtub in here was used in Hollywood Roman epics. I haggled my own self with a junk dealer for it. So I would be more than delighted to help you take a bath in it," Marilyn said.

"Well, if you insist," Jessica said, smiling at Marilyn. She led the way into the bathroom.

Marilyn undressed first, donning one of the bathrobes hanging in the closet. Jessica closed her eyes as Marilyn began undressing her, peeling away the blouse, unzipping her slacks. The cotton camisole came next and then her panties and last, Marilyn unhooked Jessica's brassiere and cupped the swells in her hands.

"I've tried to forget how your skin feels," Marilyn murmured, "but it is just as soft as I remember." She gently propelled Jessica into the cool water, and turned on a low setting of the underwater jets. "If you lie back right here, you can almost fall asleep and not worry about the water at all."

"Oh, this *is* heaven," Jessica breathed, her feet floating in the cool water as she lay back. The jets pulsed softly against her thighs and back. Her shoulders rested comfortably in a niche.

Marilyn went into the main room and came back with the cart. She sat down on the edge of the tub and began feeding Jessica strawberries and peaches dipped in the cream. After a while Jessica sat more upright, thoroughly relaxed and thoroughly prepared to get very, very intimate. It felt right, so easy, so good. She couldn't deny it. She didn't want to deny what she felt — not any more.

She sipped the brandy, feeling the heat of it burn down to her toes. It was as if she were drinking electricity in contrast to the cool water. She felt the prickle of its potency in her nipples, between her legs. Eyes closed, she opened her mouth for another strawberry and instead received Marilyn's lips brushing against hers.

Jessica felt her passion exploding as a fire flashing through her. Marilyn's mouth was warm and inviting, eager and alluring. Without hesitation, Marilyn stepped out of her robe and Jessica's eyes didn't leave her as Marilyn went to the steps leading down into the water.

She fell back to appreciate Marilyn's body as she stepped gracefully down the steps. She was the perfectly balanced combination of beautiful features:

item, Betty Grable legs; item, Racquel Welch breasts; item, Marilyn Monroe derriere; item. . . . Jessica gave up her cataloging as Marilyn relaxed onto one of the underwater shelves and lay back. Her breasts were above the water and Jessica slowly, deliberately tasted each. Marilyn wound her arms around Jessica and pulled their bodies firmly together.

She slowly moved down Marilyn's body. Marilyn slid back up out of the tub to lie on the edge and Jessica floated between the long legs. Her lips went to Marilyn's blond tufts, her tongue seeking to part Marilyn, to drink the passion she knew she would find.

Marilyn gasped and pulled Jessica into her, then fell back, arching, arms flung out to either side. Jessica breathed in deeply, savoring the taste and smell of Marilyn's sweetness. It warmed her far more powerfully than the brandy. When Marilyn cried out and went limp Jessica went limp as well, clinging to Marilyn's legs, breathless.

Marilyn sat up slowly and pulled Jessica up out of the water into her arms. Jessica let her head fall back and her mouth opened to permit Marilyn's seeking, the pressure of Marilyn's lips making her quiver.

Stretching her out on the thick rug, Marilyn toweled Jessica, starting with her feet, toweling and rubbing, massaging, slowly working up her calves and thighs, over her stomach. Marilyn paused, chasing drops on Jessica's breasts with her tongue.

With graceful ease, Jessica rolled over Marilyn, locking her mouth in a deep kiss. With a gentle wrestle, Marilyn rolled on top again and resumed toweling her. Jessica stretched and coiled around her, soaking in the luxuriousness of being massaged from head to toe. She closed her eyes and let Marilyn's mouth wander over her.

A flick of a warm tongue over her stomach, soft lips pressing on her thighs, a hint of teeth rasping over one nipple. She felt a swelling heat rising in her body. Each touch of Marilyn's mouth to another part of her made her tingle and tremble. Finally Marilyn's hands brushed where her mouth had been, lightly at first, then with more pressure, more warmth.

Marilyn settled beside her, her breasts pressed into Jessica's side, and one firm finger began tracing down Jessica's body, over her shoulders, between her breasts, down her stomach, headed for Jessica's heat and wetness. It slid between Jessica's legs, entering her, immersed in flowing passion. As her center parted, her mouth parted and a soft sound of delight and desire escaped her. Jessica pulled Marilyn's mouth down to kiss her again, feeling the pleasure building between them. She sighed deeply as Marilyn stroked her, sliding, brushing, letting Jessica grab at her, pulling the pleasure deep within her.

Yes, yes, yes, she chanted to Herself. This is what I want!

Yes! Jessica clung to Marilyn's softness and shuddered as orgasm rippled through her.

There was more brandy, more bathing, more lovemaking. Much later, alone with her notes, Jessica was unable to concentrate. Every moment with Marilyn had been exquisite, but there was a strange feeling in the pit of her stomach. She was ambivalent, scared.

Restlessly, she paced in front of the window, only partially appreciating the San Antonio nightfall. Okay, she was a lesbian, and Marilyn was a lesbian. Was she falling in love with Marilyn?

Oh come off it, Herself protested. You just can't be happy, can you? You finally admit to the truth and now you want it all. You want to be In Love. When are you going to grow up?

She ignored the question and studied her notes, reviewing her opening remarks several times. After dark she went for a brisk walk along the Riverwalk, then back to her room to watch the news, which was uninspiring as usual. Did anybody really care if Skylab re-entered Earth's atmosphere? She ignored the TV and dozed, telling Herself she should get up and go to bed.

There were soft lights and soft music, a soft touch and soft murmurs. They seemed to surround her as she wandered among outstretched arms that were caressing, calling, desiring her. She was tempted to give way to each, to enjoy the varied pleasures, steep in their sensuality. But she searched on for a particular face, a particular body, a particular smile.

Her heart pounding, Jessica jerked out of her doze, her back cramped. She hadn't meant to fall asleep in the chair . . . what a strange half-waking dream.

I wonder when I'll stop thinking about sex all the time, she asked Herself. I wonder if the news in any city will ever be worth watching? I wonder if I should mention Letitia Baldrige's new book tomorrow?

* * * * *

The first day's programs went very well, and she was able to relax and enjoy lecturing. The only rough spot in the day had come when she tried to tactfully explain to the class of saleswomen from all over the United States about too much makeup. Several of the women had vocally resented Jessica's statement about the difference between models and professionals.

"Maybe if I give you an example. My neighbor is a very attractive woman. She used to be a model. She noticed one day that she wasn't closing her own sales. She'd get to a certain point and then clients would ask to see her boss before they'd sign. She realized it was a common problem for all women like her — dressed up-to-the-minute fashion-wise, chic hair, dazzling eye makeup. But the more conservatively dressed women, the ones who still dressed sharply — showed they had flair and style in small ways, but wore very little makeup — those women didn't have that problem. They closed their own sales. They kept all their commissions that way.

"So she started wearing just foundation, blusher and a hint of eye makeup. She went to a simple but sophisticated hair style and kept it the same from day to day. And she started closing her own sales. Clients stopped triple-checking facts with her, or going to her boss. She told me it still goes on . . . Yes, did you have a question?"

"No, not a question," said a well-dressed woman with an understated elegance. "An observation. What you're saying goes on in my company too. All our client representatives are male, every single one. And some of them will work with a female sales rep for a couple of months then suddenly ask to see me or my boss before signing. I couldn't figure it out. The attractive women in my unit got the most contacts, and they got to the final draft a lot quicker than I did. But they didn't get the signatures at my rate. Well, one day, in front of me, this one client told my boss how smart he was to use such terrific 'bait.' *Then* the answer hit me. The clients didn't take the really pretty women in my unit seriously. When I told one of my friends about it she was really upset. It isn't fair to her that her looks work against her, but at least she realizes the score now. Now she plays down her looks."

"Thank you," Jessica said sincerely, "that's very helpful to me. I agree, it just isn't fair to be evaluated on your looks, but think about it — if you see a client in a polyester suit you immediately assume he's a jerk, right? Right. Same client, pinstripes, he just might be okay, right? So why is it such a surprise that the client looks at your makeup, a part of your attire, and decides, based on what he or she sees, that you're either smart or sexy." She smiled and her voice took on a sarcastic edge. "Everybody knows the two can't possibly go together, right?" She received several smiles of comprehension in return.

"Maybe if I give you one more example. I'm working with a software company right now. I've been asking existing clients why they went with the company's services, trying to weed out those decision factors that relate exclusively to sales techniques. Well, I've also talked to clients the company lost. One

67

of them told me that *he* decided not to go with the company because the sales rep didn't know what *she* was talking about.

"That explanation really surprised me, because the company prides itself on its really excellent training for all salespeople. So I talked to the rep in question. It took me about two seconds to figure out what had happened. She had fingernails so long she made a lot of mistakes when she used a keyboard during her product demonstration. The client interpreted her clumsiness as lack of product knowledge, probably while he was thinking her fingernails looked great. Her attractive hands cost her the client, and the company lost the account."

She saw the light go on in several faces. She hid a smile while several women surreptitiously examined their fingernails.

"In my observation, men generally want us to dress in one of two ways. One, they want us to dress *sexy* so they're constantly aware we are women. That gives them the perfect excuse to go on treating us like wives and mistresses, not equals. Or, on the other extreme, they would like us to dress so they are able to forget we *are* women. I guess some men prefer us sexless, along the lines of mothers, daughters or sisters, so they can rest assured that their hormones, which have no place in the business relationship, won't act up. Personally, I don't think either extreme guarantees success for any but a few exceptional women. There must be at least a third way for the vast majority of us to dress, a way in which we can still have the respect and trust of those we deal with without sacrificing our female selves.

"Let's start with something simple. The way we

stand, especially in heels. Everybody stand up and we'll learn how to unlock our poor mistreated knees." The speed with which the women stood was gratifying and Jessica was inordinately pleased.

By evening, she was riding high, not even minding her aching feet or tired throat. Exhaustion would catch up to her on the plane trip home as it always did but she had tonight and another session to manage. She would get through both all on adrenaline as usual.

"How are things with you?" Marilyn asked quietly as they strolled side by side through the crowds on the Riverwalk after dinner. "I meant to ask yesterday, but somehow we didn't talk very much."

"I noticed," Jessica said with a smile. "I'm doing just fine. There are another two engagements next month and I'm negotiating with a publisher for a book."

"You've decided to publish at last?"

"At last . . . it seems the thing to do. Actually I decided to do it because almost anyone with a degree is getting published these days, and a lot of the advice is pure garbage. In some cases it's downright damaging. One book I just finished stated categorically that women should *never* wear long hair and *never* wear anything lighter than dark charcoal. The list of 'don'ts' was worse than in *Dress for Success*. I'm tired of books telling women they always need to dress, think and act like men to gain respect."

"I'm glad you're going to write your theories down. Your mind is what first attracted me to you, you know. I thought I'd find out what kind of lectures we were having in our hotel and slipped in.

You were talking about assessing situations and using particular methods to resolve conflict. I've used some of them."

Jessica was profoundly pleased. "Why, thank you. That means a lot, coming from you. Anyway, the publisher wants me to keep politics out of the book. We're negotiating that. I'm perfectly willing to leave public policy out of it, but the publisher's definition is really the politics of female/male relationships outside of the workplace. I don't see how I can just ignore the other two-thirds of women's lives."

"You can't. The way you operate successfully in business, making your expectations clear, setting performance standards for yourself and your co-workers, listening to others and compromising, doing what's expected of you — all that applies to home just as much as the office. If it's an equal relationship," Marilyn said firmly.

"That's what I told them."

"Hmmm. Maybe we should stay out of the bedroom altogether. I enjoy talking to you," Marilyn said seriously.

"I enjoy talking to you, too," Jessica said with a sober smile. "Sometimes I wonder. . . ." Her voice trailed off.

"Wonder what?" Marilyn asked when Jessica hesitated. "Come on, you've given me lots of free advice over the past year. I've enjoyed knowing you, both in and out of bed. Talk to me." She leaned against a stone wall between the walk and the canal and looked directly into Jessica's eyes, serious, waiting for her to go on.

"You're going to think I'm an awful fool," Jessica said. "I think I'll slip in your estimation a little.

70

After all, I'm Jessica the answer woman." Marilyn just smiled slightly and waited for her to continue. "Just recently I've come to realize my only sexual desires are . . . for . . . well, you know."

"No, I don't," Marilyn said. "Jessie, you're not going to tell me something disgusting about animals and peanut butter, are you?"

Jessica laughed. "No, I guess it's really not that bad. I love women."

"Yes?"

"Well, I just figured out what that makes me. I never thought of myself that way before."

"Jessica!" Marilyn turned to Jessica and took her hands. "You're a lesbian, like me, like the women you've been with! Haven't you ever come out?"

"No." Her voice was just a whisper. "I'm scared, Marilyn."

"My God. I have been marveling at how you've made a very special relationship with women a part of yourself. I wanted to be more like you," Marilyn said. Then, in a wondering voice, she said, "And you've never come out?"

"Those are the major buzz words these days, coming out. What do they mean, Marilyn?" Jessica asked with a mixture of bitterness and bewilderment. "What is coming out? What will be different? What's going to happen to me?"

"Coming out is what you make it. Look, when I came out it was, oh ten years ago, in sixty-eight. I had just broken up with my long-time beau. I decided my life was not going to include men. I was going to be a loner. I was going to build an incredible ivory tower and live in it. Well, I found out there is a lot of pressure when a pretty woman decides to be alone.

71

I was immediately treated like some sort of freak. I don't think plain women have that problem. It's both easier and harder on them."

"I think I know what you mean. Beautiful Marilyn gets asked why a pretty woman like her doesn't like men. Ordinary Jessica, on the other hand, is probably unmarried because she hasn't gotten lucky. I'm an object of pity, but not a freak like you."

"That's it," Marilyn said. "That's what I run into all the time. Well, it was pretty hard to take being called a freak just because I wanted to be alone. I found myself drawn to other solitary women so I wouldn't be thought of as a loner anymore. And one day I admitted to myself that I wanted them, these wonderful, vibrant women — to be part of their energy, to share my own. That was the day I came out. I just told myself officially what I'd suspected for so long. You don't have to take out a full-page ad."

"I'm not sure about what I want," Jessica said, a little despairingly.

"Nobody will know better than you. My God, I just can't imagine you're what you are, as incredible as you are in bed, and you haven't realized it's your life."

"I know, Marilyn, I know I was just kidding myself about someday finding a man and settling down. It was an illusion of normality I clung to — a remnant of my upbringing, I guess. I just lived my life without ever saying I want to be with women. But I'm still afraid, tied up in knots."

Marilyn led the way further along the Riverwalk. "Tell me about your fear."

"Like I'm afraid right now someone will overhear

us and whisper about me and point and stare. That clients will stop using me and associations will stop hiring me to speak."

"I understand that kind of fear. But you must be what you are. Can you really go through life limited, just half of yourself? You're secure in your profession. Don't you owe other women who aren't as secure your commitment to prove you can overcome society?"

"But you don't advertise you're a, a . . . lesbian." Jessica found it very hard to say the word.

"Of course not. Unfortunately, saying lesbian puts your sex life on the table, and I think talking about sex with casual acquaintances is in bad taste. If I thought people would understand what lesbian really means — I mean it's more than just sex, so much more — well then I'd tell everyone I meet, in the same way you'd tell someone you're married, or you're Catholic or a vegetarian. It's a . . . sureness, a philosophy."

"I wish I could be like you, so unafraid," Jessica whispered, stopping to look over the canal. The raucous music from a Mexican bar drifted in the air, giving Jessica a feeling of being at carnivaál. Nothing was real.

"Down here I run into an occasional jackass who insists I'm some kind of freak." Marilyn took a deep breath. "It makes me angry, and frightened, and I usually bundle myself up in sunglasses and a leather jacket and go to our dyke bar and get drunk. There actually is one in San Antonio. This isn't San Francisco, we don't have a gay . . . what's his name, Harvey Milk, on the City Council. Our council pretends our bar doesn't exist. And while I'm drinking I think to myself, that asshole doesn't know

73

the half of it. Wouldn't he die if he came here and saw all these strong women? And I laugh to myself. Someday, we'll break free and remake this world of ours. Someday!" Marilyn made a fist and Jessica felt a strange thrill.

She remembered her first speech long ago, during college.

She had been called an activist, a libber, a bitch-on-wheels, and it hadn't mattered. She'd had friends, and the women's center. And now she didn't. Was that the difference? Was she just feeling very alone?

"What brings up this question now?" Marilyn asked. "You've lived this way for years."

"I don't know. I suddenly realized people could be calling me a name I didn't understand and had never applied to myself. Instinctively I think of lesbian as a bad word. But when I look at my life, your life, I think we're beautiful to be free." Tears in her eyes, she shook her head. "But I've been realizing I'm not free from the world and responsibilities to my — kind. I'm feeling very alone. I've unintentionally turned my back on a world I desperately want to be a part of."

"Well, let's go, then," Marilyn said.

"Where?"

"To the Queen of Cups bookstore. It's not far." Marilyn set off back toward the hotel.

They drove around the block and Jessica saw the sign as Marilyn parked the car. QUEEN OF CUPS BOOKS. A WOMEN'S COOPERATIVE.

"Marilyn, I can't," Jessica said.

"Nobody's going to take your picture. Besides, it's not a lesbian bookstore, it's a woman's bookstore. If you're on the front page tomorrow, you can say truthfully that you *are* a woman."

"Uh —"

"Come on," she said. She got out of the car and went around to Jessica's door.

Jessica got out and put her hands in her pockets.

"You look as if you're going in front of a firing squad," Marilyn said.

"That's what I feel like."

They went in the front door. Marilyn said hello to the tall black woman who was reading *In Our Own Words* as she sat next to the cash register. I wonder if she's a lesbian, Jessica asked Herself.

"This way," Marilyn said.

They wandered among the shelves. Science fiction, philosophy, poetry, child rearing, medical guides — and everything oriented to women. Jessica stopped occasionally to look at a book.

They turned a corner and Marilyn came to a stop. "Take your pick," she said.

Lesbian books. Books about making love, books about coming out, books about being Lesbian mothers, books about self-awareness. Slowly, Jessica pulled a book off the shelf.

"Jessica, the last book you need to read right now is *The Well of Loneliness*," Marilyn said firmly. "Put it back."

"I read it in college," Jessica said.

"Look for something a trifle more self-affirming," Marilyn said. She drifted away to the other end of the shelves.

Jessica's finger ran over the spines of books. *Desert of the Heart.* She had heard of it. She pulled it off the shelf and read the flyleaf.

"I really enjoyed that," someone said. Jessica jumped and whirled to face the speaker.

It was the black woman from the counter. She smiled pleasantly at Jessica. "If you liked that, you should try this one," she said, pulling *Patience and Sarah* from the shelf.

"Thanks," Jessica managed. I'm talking to a real, live, admitted lesbian, she told Herself. She felt her face flush bright red, right up to the roots of her hair. Her mouth opened and closed like a fish.

The woman looked at her in concern and put her strong, supporting hand on Jessica's arm. "I'm sorry —"

"Don't worry," Marilyn said, joining them. "It's her first time."

"Oh," the woman said as comprehension dawned. She smiled broadly. "Well, it has to be your first time some time."

Jessica hid her face behind the books, laughing. "Christ, but I'm being stupid."

Marilyn hugged her. The woman said, "It's okay. Contrary to popular belief, not all of us were born gay. It takes a little getting used to."

Jessica laughed again and peered at Marilyn from behind her books. "I think I have two books I want," she said.

She paid for her books, thanking the woman again, and they drove back to the hotel. Marilyn guided the car gracefully into her parking place.

"Well, what did you think?"

Jessica took a deep breath. "I wish I'd realized this sooner, come to terms with it sooner. Maybe then you and I —"

"Jess, don't," Marilyn said with a sigh that had a gulp in it.

"Why not?" Jessica turned to Marilyn and caught her hand, smiling, feeling lightheaded. "Maybe we didn't screw up a perfectly wonderful friendship by making love that first night."

"Darlin'," and Marilyn's voice grew very soft, very tender, "I thought about you for a long time last night. And I asked myself what might have happened if we'd become friends first, gotten to trust each other, become really involved with each other's thoughts and lives, and then made love. Maybe I'd be trying to open another hotel in San Francisco and not New York. Maybe everything would be different." She pulled the keys out of the ignition and stared at them, avoiding Jessica's eyes.

There was a hard, painful lump in Jessica's throat. After a while Marilyn got out of the car. Jessica followed her into the hotel and up to her room. When the door closed, Marilyn kissed her lovingly.

Jessica pulled back. "Is it too late?" she asked, her throat aching, her voice scratchy with emotion.

"Our lives are too different."

"And yet so similar," Jessica whispered back.

Marilyn held Jessica against her and then sighed deeply. "I've done something to you I don't believe in, and I couldn't help myself," she said sadly, her drawl becoming more pronounced. "You're the sun, Jessica, and I wanted to bask in you. But, I . . . I'm very much in love, as I understand what love means, with another woman. And I'm here with you, adoring every minute, even considering how I might be with you more often."

To Jessica, the room seemed to go dark. For a moment she was violently angry at being cheated and lied to, and then she just felt empty. Marilyn was one of the women in her little black book. She had never expected any of them to be faithful — they were all one-night stands. She went to the bedroom to bury her face in a pillow, more distraught over her sudden emptiness than at anything Marilyn had said.

Marilyn followed her saying, "I'm sorry, Jessie, but it's the truth. I shouldn't be here with you, not by all that's sacred, but I am, and even as we talk I'm thinking about loving you again."

"Don't, Marilyn, please don't. I'm so confused. Just hold me," she pleaded and Marilyn lay down on the bed with her, rocking her, stroking her curly hair, murmuring nothing in particular.

"I know I'm not in love with you," Jessica said with an air of finality. "I was blinded by a beautiful picture of loving someone so much that we could always be together. I don't even think you were in that picture. It was so radiant and I think —" she drew in a long, shuddering breath, "I've discovered loneliness."

"Oh, darlin'," was all Marilyn said as she kept rocking Jessica.

"What's she like?" Jessica asked a little later, trying to draw out of the despondency she could feel taking over her. Okay, now that I've decided I'm a lesbian, and now that I've decided I want a permanent relationship, what am I to do? Herself was silent.

"Tall and lanky, completely unlike you. She's gentle and quiet and she teaches children and is so very good to me. She lives in Corpus Christi and I go

78

there on the weekends. We've been seeing each other for almost four years. I know she wishes we could be together all the time, but I just can't bring myself to ask her to move in with me, even though I know she would give up her life in Corpus Christi in a second if I asked. I treasure my freedom too much, and I don't know if I can accept that kind of sacrifice from her. But I do love her. I look forward to every weekend. When I can't make it there I fret, when we come together after a few weeks apart it's as if we're rediscovering our love."

"And yet you want to be with other women?" Jessica asked in confusion.

"No, I want to be with you. Even when I call you I feel as though I'm cheating on her. I told you, you're like the sun," Marilyn said gently. "I feel as if I have the seven year itch. I try not to think about it at all."

"I try that too. When I'm home, I don't think about Chicago, or Boston, or San Antonio. I just think about my work. But it's impossible to be schizophrenic all the time. I've got to start being what I am."

"I know, I know. I love her, I really do."

Marilyn's arms closed around Jessica, holding her tighter. A chill rippled through Jessica and then she was holding Marilyn's mouth against hers, and pulling frantically at their clothes.

They made love in a hurried and fevered rush of fingers and mouths. When it was over she heard Marilyn whisper good-bye. She fell into a dark and murky sleep, full of dark and murky dreams.

SIX
Long, Hot Summer

Jessica couldn't work. She'd been assembling material for a new lecture series, thinking about maybe lecturing at Golden Gate or San Francisco State, instead of being on the road so much. She'd watched Bjorn Borg win Wimbledon again. She had to admit that for a man he was pretty mesmerizing to watch. She'd done some preliminary work on the book. The publisher wanted a firm publication date. She didn't know what to say.

The summer was endless. When the weather wasn't foggy it was too warm and she felt limp, like a hothouse plant. She no longer hesitated in thinking of herself as a lesbian. Now she was miserable about being alone.

She knew of at least one women's bookstore in the vicinity. Her two books from San Antonio had been inspiring and stirring, but she still found she lacked the courage to go alone, something Herself found quite unfathomable.

It's not you who has to go in, she told Herself, but Me.

But you'd meet some nice women, Herself said. Some passionate women, too.

But I can't use a women's bookstore as a pick-up place.

Well then don't, Herself snapped. Pretend you're a deaf-mute. You could at least buy some more books.

They are getting dog-eared, she mused. So she went, bought books, looked at the new records, and left again. When spoken to, she was pleasant in return, but nothing more. Finding the sort of relationship she wanted took energy and time. She didn't feel settled enough to even begin.

Those short trips brought her a rich re-awakening, though, as she discovered her feminism again. She was interested in politics again. And there was so much going on in San Francisco, she found that after years of apathy she was concerned about the issues. The Briggs Initiative had qualified for the November ballot and suddenly San Francisco was the center of the controversy.

She read the papers every day, following every article about the growing gay and lesbian rights movement in San Francisco. Coalitions were springing up to contest the idea that people should be barred from certain professions based on personal preferences, the most vocal of which were led by Harvey Milk. But the Briggs Initiative was worse than she had first supposed — the proposed law went further. It also said that straight people who advocated (or maybe just tolerated) homosexuality should not be allowed to teach in public schools either.

She admired Harvey Milk as she watched him not just speak out, but demand that others who had been silent speak out too. He urged all gay and lesbian people to step forward and be counted. He made her feel guilty for not being open about her sexuality. He wasn't afraid — and San Francisco was changing for the better.

But she was still afraid. She kept her fear, her concern, and her sexuality, hidden from the rest of the world, especially Cat.

Watching the political scene heat up with the summer, Jessica found concentrating on work a strain. She went to movies alone mostly because Cat was often not at home in the evenings. She tried to not think about where Cat might be. She toyed with her word processor, playing games, spending hours organizing the work she hadn't started and really had no heart to do.

One afternoon there was a crash outside her door and she went to investigate, suspecting that Cat had dropped her groceries again while she fished for her keys. "At least it wasn't the eggs," Jessica said with a laugh, retrieving an errant onion and two escaping carrots.

Cat giggled and managed to get the door unlocked. "I knew this load wasn't going to make it, but I told myself I was setting a new world's record for amount of groceries carried up three floors in one trip. The elevator's on the fritz and I'm in a terrible rush. This tomato is history. The butter fell on it." Cat frowned as she collected the carrots and onion from Jessica.

"Anything I can do to help?"

"I need to change my clothes. Can you dice onions or peel carrots?"

"I think so," Jessica said. She'd give it her best shot. Lingering here was better than going home and staring at the blank screen.

Cat reappeared several minutes later. She had traded her lovely lavender suit for a pair of slacks and overblouse of a brilliant rose. Jessica thought Cat was more blonde and fair than ever. She had never noticed Cat's shoulders before, either. They were firm, and strong, but yielding, too. Perfect for laying your head on — she stopped her wandering thoughts.

"Thanks, I think I'll take over now," Cat said, tying an apron over her outfit.

"You're welcome. I'll make myself scarce." Cat obviously had a hot date which was just as well. Herself observed that Jessica definitely didn't need to spend any more time with Cat at the moment.

She opened Cat's door and found herself face to face with a very good-looking man. At least she supposed he was good looking, if you liked bronze and brawny. She looked him over as she called to Cat, "Someone's here to see you."

"Already? Oh my gosh. You're early," Cat said to the man as she came out of the kitchen. "Jessica, this is Paul, Paul, Jessica."

Jessica exchanged pleasantries and then went home. That must be Paul the Jerk, she told Herself. She had thought Cat was through with him but apparently he was making a come-back bid. Cat had described him as self-centered and macho, and completely unable to treat Cat as anything but a child. Which was how he had looked to her.

What's it to you, anyway, Herself asked as Jessica picked out a suit for tomorrow's one-day trip to Los Angeles. Cat is perfectly free to make up her mind, and make her own mistakes.

She ignored this important point, and concentrated on her reflection. She tried on a new blouse and decided it matched the somewhat avant garde pale rose suit she had just bought. The rose suit looked odd in among all the black, gray and navy blue. It was her conscious effort to emphasize to herself and to others that she was not a cookie-cutter conformist — at least not anymore.

She looked at her body in the mirror. "Saddlebags. Hmph." But very soft saddlebags, she added, and after a moment she lay down on the bed, thinking about sex, wondering if she'd ever make love again.

She had burned her little black book. Being alone was better than a relationship with anyone who wasn't prepared for a more lasting commitment. That much had changed in her life. Herself reminded Jessica talk was easy. Wait until you've been without sex for two years, Herself said.

She'd been to Boston but hadn't called Elaine, nor had she called Roberta when she'd been in Chicago. She'd gone to see Gina sing in New York, but hadn't

84

looked her up afterwards. She was horny a lot, and disgusted with Herself. She had thought she could live without sex.

"You should have called Elaine," she murmured, "you should have. You would have loved it, she would have loved it. You're both free agents." She'd thought the same thing when she was in Boston but had never picked up the phone.

She remembered the little pub Elaine co-owned, remembered how she had caught Elaine looking at her, evaluating her body. And she remembered how she had moved her body in response, letting Elaine know she didn't mind.

At closing time, Jessica had taken her time. When almost everyone else had gone, she had asked Elaine if it would be easy to hail a cab, or if she should call for one.

"Where are you headed?" Elaine had asked and then she'd said Jessica could walk there quite safely. Elaine had then offered to walk along because it was on her way home.

Jessica trailed her hands over her stomach and breasts, remembering the way they had talked about nothing, and then when they were in the dark shadow of a building how they had turned to each other and kissed.

Jessica groaned, envisioning Elaine undressing her, the feel of her short red hair against her thighs, the simple ecstasy they had shared. Remembering, fantasizing, was all Jessica had.

The doorbell rang. With a gasp, only moments away from orgasm, Jessica started up off the bed. She grabbed her robe and went to the door.

Cat was wiping her hands on her apron and looking frantic. "Were you going to take a bath, gosh I'm sorry," she said. "I forgot to buy garlic."

"It's okay, I hadn't started running the water yet," Jessica assured her, trying to hide how flustered she was. Then she laughed. "What on earth makes you think I have garlic?"

"I was praying. Silly of me."

Jessica shut the door and led Cat to the kitchen. "Hmmm. I wonder what's in here." Jessica hunted through a cupboard, pulling out a variety of containers, some marked, some holding ancient mysteries.

"Ugh! Oh, Jessica, really." Cat had cracked open a container and was now holding it out at arm's length.

"I think that's some old Parmesan cheese."

"Old isn't the word. Didn't you throw this kind of thing out when you moved?"

"I never had the chance. And I was afraid to look inside."

Cat made a derisive noise. "Is there garlic or not?"

"There's this." Jessica proffered a container of garlic salt.

"No real garlic?"

"Isn't it the same thing?"

"No, it isn't the same thing," Cat informed her haughtily. "Just like cabernet and thunderbird are not the same thing."

"Well, does garlic keep forever?"

"Almost."

"There might be some in this old cookie jar, hang on," Jessica said, climbing up onto the counter. She reached into the back of the top shelf. "Ah ha!" She handed Cat the jar.

Cat yelped as the jar slid through her fingers and smashed on the floor. "Don't jump down!" she ordered. "There's glass everywhere — oh merde! Are you cut?"

"No, I'm fine. I couldn't help it," Jessica gasped. She didn't want to look at her foot.

"Get back on the counter. Oh, you did cut yourself," Cat moaned. "It's all my fault."

"Don't be silly. It's just a little cut."

Cat continued to mutter while she found the broom and swept the shards into a paper bag. "Stay there," she ordered when Jessica began to climb off the counter. "Okay, keep your foot off the ground and lean on my shoulder."

Jessica tried to keep her foot up, but she was also acutely aware of her robe beginning to come untied. She felt hot and fevered where her body was pressed against Cat's.

They hobbled to the sofa and Cat sat down on the coffee table, putting Jessica's foot in her lap. "Oh yuck, there's a piece in it, come on, we've got to get to the bathroom and rinse it out. It's really not too bad, just bloody."

"You're getting blood on your outfit. It'll never come out of silk and it's so lovely on you," Jessica bemoaned.

"Oh, pooh. Come on."

They managed to get Jessica's foot under the faucet, but only with considerable coordination from a one-legged Jessica trying to keep her body covered, and from petite Cat trying to keep them from falling. She bit her lower lip and blinked back tears as the water stung the cut. It didn't hurt that much, but the cut was still very sensitive.

"Come on, lie down and I'll bandage it up. I received a Merit Badge for first aid," Cat said, swabbing carefully at the cut with peroxide. She bound a wad of Kleenex wrapped in a layer of gauze to Jessica's foot with masking tape, tsking the whole time. Jessica concentrated on Cat's lively description of Girl Scouting as she lay on her stomach, painfully aware of the thinness of her robe. She could feel the warmth of Cat's breath on her damp foot. It felt good to be cared for.

"I don't want you to get up. Leave your foot elevated so the bleeding stops. I'll check back on you in a couple of hours."

"A couple of hours? I can't lie here that long!"

"What do you need? I'll bring it here."

"The book from my office, and today's paper on the coffee table and a glass of water."

Cat brought them all and then left, saying, "I'm leaving the door unlocked, and I'm taking the garlic salt."

Jessica tried to read and then she worried about being able to get to L.A. in the morning. The meeting was a university advisory committee for the women's studies program. She didn't want to miss the meeting because of the contacts she made. The terminals were a long walk, but maybe if she dug out the cane she'd used when she'd broken her ankle a couple of years ago she could manage.

The room began to grow dark but she didn't feel like turning on the light to read. In fact, her bed was rather warm and cozy and she drifted, thinking about the future, dreaming about the past.

"Hey, Jessica, wake up," someone was saying. She stirred a little then opened her eyes.

"Cat," she whispered softly, dazedly wondering what Cat was doing in her bedroom.

"Come to check your foot, pardner." Cat peeled off the masking tape she'd used to bind the gauze to Jessica's foot. "It's stopped bleeding. I brought some real gauze and tape."

Jessica tried to hide her shiver as Cat lifted her foot and sat down on the bed. Cat's hands were gentle and warm and Jessica closed her eyes.

She was making a big mistake, and she knew it even as she did it, but she imagined Cat was always going to be there, that Cat would wrap her foot, then lie down next to her and hold her, and kiss her and make everything better. Cat's lips must be very soft, she told Herself. Cat's body must be so very passionate, she imagined. She shut her ears to the warnings Herself was shouting — something about straight women and heartache.

"You feeling okay?" Cat asked.

"Sure. I'm just sleepy." She sat, not really caring that her robe was starting to open, wanting Cat to see her body, wanting Cat to want her.

"Don't get up," Cat ordered. She looked flushed from her exertions. "And you probably shouldn't do a lot of walking tomorrow."

Reason returned and Jessica settled back on the bed. She was a fool. She took a deep breath to clear her head. "Sorry, I'm flying to L.A. for the day. But I have a cane and I'll be careful."

"Well, okay. If your foot starts to bleed again you should have it looked at. Maybe you should anyway."

"I'll keep an eye on it."

"Here, let me help you get under the covers."

"No, really, I can manage," Jessica protested. She had nothing on under her robe and now she desperately didn't want Cat to see her. She felt as if desire were written all over her.

"Come on, don't be silly. I'll arrange the pillows around your foot so you can elevate it. You can't do it yourself."

Jessica continued to protest, but Cat overruled her. The robe slid off her shoulders and Cat drew back a little as Jessica attempted to nonchalantly cover her breasts with it.

"Where do you keep your nightgowns?"

"I, uh, I usually don't wear one. One of the benefits of living alone," Jessica mumbled.

"I know what you mean." Impersonally, Cat pulled Jessica's robe away as she slid between the sheets and then Cat put a pillow under her foot. She tensed as Cat arranged more pillows around her foot to keep the sheets from pressing too hard on it and Cat's hands brushed over her calves and ankles.

"More water?" Cat asked.

"No, I'm fine. Thank you," Jessica said as Cat flicked off the light. She couldn't see Cat's face anymore.

"What are friends for?" Cat emphasized *friends* with a laugh Jessica thought sounded strained. "Paul will wonder what's kept me. Sleep well. Be careful tomorrow."

She waited until she heard the door close and then she buried her face deep into the pillow, wrapping her arms around it. Fool, you complete fool, she cursed Herself. Why Cat? You're not in love with her, you're just horny! Stop thinking about her, stop it!

She tried to remember making love with Marilyn, and she filled her ears with the sound of Marilyn's voice on the telephone.

Do you want to lose a friend? You know she doesn't care for you that way, she's straight, Herself said emphatically. Herself reminded Jessica that she had been warned.

There was Roberta, Roberta's mouth, she remembered, and for a while the memory distracted her. Eventually she fell asleep.

The alarm jarred her awake what seemed like only minutes later and she fumbled for the snooze button.

"Oh lord, oh lord, oh lord, get up," she muttered aloud, "gotta get on a plane, come on." After a moment she remembered why she was sleeping on her stomach and she gave her foot a few preliminary twists. So far so good.

She took a shower and taped some more gauze to the bottom of her foot and added an extra layer for padding. It still took forever to get dressed and finally she practiced with the cane on her way to the kitchen. She got out some yogurt and opened the blinds.

The yogurt tasked like wallpaper paste. The sun was dim and unfriendly. It was a wretched day, she told Herself, just a wretched day. Her black mood had nothing to do with the fact that from her window she had seen the bronze and brawny Paul getting into his car in his clothes he had been in last night.

91

It's got nothing to do with you, you fool!

She limped down the three flights of stairs, holding her head up high, telling Herself it didn't matter. Life went on.

SEVEN
The Fine Art of Self-Torture &
Other Diversions

Jessica finally began the book in earnest, pulling together the four or five existing theories about male/female roles in the workplace she liked, while finally committing her own to paper.

It took a lot of research and reading, which was just as well, because by working hard she didn't spend any time counting the number of times a week

Paul visited Cat, nor the number of times she noticed Cat coming home in the morning to change on her way to work.

She communed daily with her word processor, setting up reference files and endless footnote material which she would glean for content when she sat down to begin actually writing. After several hours she would take a break, play word processor hangman, and then go back to work.

Cat was available to go to the movies, every once in a while, or they sometimes split a pizza. They saw *The Deerhunter* and *Annie Hall* and Cat insisted that Jessica see *Star Wars*. And sometimes she enjoyed the luxury of watching Cat when Cat was watching something else, studying her, noticing the crinkle around her eyes when Cat smiled. She didn't even mind that Cat would only drop by when Paul wasn't around. Jessica basked in Cat's bubbly and vivacious temperament. Cat's fire was absorbed into Jessica's coolness and Jessica rejoiced in the heat of it.

Summer came slowly to a close and she began to emerge into a new self. At least that was how matters appeared to Herself. Herself thought she was spending too much on clothes, but when Cat mentioned that she thought Jessica should wear brighter blues and greens, she had felt compelled to take her advice.

Cat's modern and dramatic tastes made inroads into Jessica's life, and she let the changes happen. They went to an art deco exhibit and a rather odd concert without musical instruments that she actually found she enjoyed. She even wallpapered one wall in her bedroom. Whether the new Jessica was the result of Cat or not, she dated her new life from the first time she and Cat had gone out. Everything else was B.C. — Before Cat. She knew she would regret letting the time she had shared with Cat mean so much.

But sometimes when they sat in one or the other's place and drank wine and ate pizza and watched a movie or a political debate, Jessica was overwhelmed with the feeling of being in sync, attuned to Cat.

"Knock it off," she said aloud, and she turned the page. After a while she sighed and gave up pretending to work. It was a pretty day so she went for a walk in Golden Gate Park, just a few blocks away.

The last of the summer flowers were fading but the grass and trees were still trying to look summer green. Jessica weaved in and out of roller skaters, walking briskly to clear her head. She went much further than she had planned and felt pleasantly tired as she unlocked her door.

The door opened opposite. "I thought I heard you. I got my tickets today," Cat said.

Jessica followed Cat into her place. She knew she shouldn't spend time with her. She knew she should have made an excuse and canceled the trip to New York, but in her heart of hearts she didn't want to. She wanted to be with Cat, even if she could never talk to or touch her the way she wanted.

Cat said, "They took your first class upgrade certificate and booked me through same as your tickets so we're all set. I could never have swung first class on my expense account so thanks a lot. I owe you a New York dinner."

"I should say so. I paid for that upgrade by listening to a bored five-year old from Salt Lake to San Antonio," Jessica said lightly. Being happy and carefree around Cat was getting harder to fake. She wanted to be intense and loving.

"Now that's an expensive upgrade," Cat said. "Want some wine?"

"What kind?"

"I've got, lemme see, cabernet and some chablis."

"Who's the cabernet by?"

"Fetzer. Seventy-six. You're so picky."

"Can't help it. Fine wine is my only vice."

"Your only vice, sure."

Jessica toyed momentarily with saying, just as a joke, "Well, fine wine and fine women," but her courage failed her. She wasn't afraid anymore of being a lesbian. But if she told Cat, she'd lose her. "Just about," Jessica said instead.

"Then how come you're always drinking my wine?" Cat demanded. "I want to see this wine cellar of yours."

They went to Jessica's place and she opened the huge walk-in closet door.

Cat gasped. "There must be a dozen cases!"

"Fourteen in all. If I find a vintage I like, I buy a case and keep it till it's ripe. The ones at the bottom are ready for imbibing."

"Hmmm, how about this zinfandel, no I want this one." Cat drew out a bottle.

"Blanc de Pinot Noir. A very fine choice, Madam. One glass coming right up."

"Just one?" Cat asked with a particularly charming smile that made Jessica swallow hard.

Maybe the fact that it was Friday night and Paul wasn't coming over made Cat seem to want to stay. Jessica kept refilling their glasses. They both got very giddy and tipsy and lay in front of the stereo listening to Jessica's favorite albums. They graduated from the pinot noir to chardonnay. They were crooning to a particularly torchy love-done-me-wrong song when Cat started talking.

"The Jerk's gone. He's history."

"Why?" Jessica asked, her heart pounding a little harder. Paul wasn't coming back. Cat was available. Her mind was fuzzy, but not so fuzzy she didn't tell Herself that nothing had altered between them.

"He said he'd changed — he told me — he swore to it, and I gave him another chance and he hadn't changed at all — he just figured out how to be more diplomatic when he was giving me this macho bullshit line about how I ought not to go out to dinner with male clients unless he was there, and about traveling by myself, and criticizing my cooking, and he kept changing jobs, and wanted to borrow money from me again. I told him to take a hike," Cat said, running out of breath.

"Goodfer you. Here's to no more macho bullshit."

"No more macho bullshit," Cat echoed and she drained her glass. "I need more wine, Jessica," she pouted and Jessica staggered to the closet for another bottle. She thought it was cabernet. Well, it was red, that much Jessica was sure of.

Cat kept talking. "He was pretty good in bed but it isn't everything not when he was such a jerk the rest of the time. I've got stannurds."

97

"Here's to standards," Jessica said, refilling both of their glasses as she sat down on the floor with a thunk.

"Here's to stannurds," Cat echoed. "Why are the guys who are great in bed always such low life?"

"I wouldn't know," Jessica said. "I've ne —"

"He was a professional sunbather. Watch out for the ones with tans. No more tans."

"Here's to no more tans," Jessica said. She knew she was very drunk and on the verge of making the BIG disclosure.

"No more tans," Cat echoed and then her voice changed. "Uh-oh."

Jessica lay very still on the floor, not at all sure she wasn't going to be just as sick as Cat. Maybe if she stayed very still she would be all right.

"I may die," Cat mumbled as she came back from the bathroom. "I should stick to cheap wine."

"No, cheap wine is even worse."

"Not for me. Did you know it's spotless behind the john?"

"Now that you mention it, no, I didn't know that."

"Well, it's spotless," Cat repeated and she stretched out on the floor again. "I wish it didn't hurt so much."

"Your head?"

"No, my heart," Cat said and her lower lip started to tremble. After a moment, two large tears overflowed the brown eyes and Jessica slid over to Cat. "Oh, Jessica," Cat said and she put her head on Jessica's chest and cried.

She cradled Cat against her breasts and closed her eyes, imagining a hundred wonderful possibilities,

98

pretending there was no Paul and no tears, that Cat would raise her lips to Jessica's.

Cat finally looked up at her, eyes bleary, lips very full. Jessica stared into Cat's eyes, getting lost in the honey brown, and she leaned very slightly toward Cat's beckoning lips, longing for just the briefest touch.

"You're a good friend, Jessica," Cat said and she closed her eyes, buried her face in Jessica's shoulder and passed out quietly.

She held her for a long time, stroking the thick blonde hair. Finally she got up the courage to lightly kiss the smooth forehead. She wiped away the traces of tears and rocked Cat. After a while Cat woke up, was sick again and then she went home "to die."

Bed welcomed her, but sleep did not. Instead, she kept slipping into a drunken daze, images of making love to Cat causing her to groan and tremble. She fantasized about kissing Cat's tantalizing lips, tasting her mouth at last. This is it, she swore. This was the last time I'm going to get drunk over Cat. Promises, promises, Herself said.

Why, now that I've figured out who I am, have I fallen for someone who's not what I am? When will I find someone who is what I am? What is love anyway? Why does red wine always leave such a bad taste in my mouth? Why do I always forget to turn off the kitchen light? Herself did not answer any of these questions.

She was sick, finally, and felt better afterwards.

* * * * *

"Come on, you'll like it, I promise. He's really funny. I can't believe you've never been here," Cat said, pulling a reluctant Jessica up a flight of stairs.

"I don't believe in comedy on demand," Jessica protested again. "I'd rather wait for the show to be on television when someone else edits out the ones who aren't funny."

"Oh, pooh. Where's your sense of adventure?" Cat gave her name to the hostess and they were escorted to one end of a long table about halfway to the stage. Jessica looked around and decided to make the best of things. She always felt so awful for the young ones. She wanted to coach them on delivery the way she'd been coached. She knew exactly what they went through when the crowd didn't respond, or — even worse — laughed politely.

"My boss is cutting my marketing budget by ten percent," Cat shared while they waited for their two-drink minimum. "I told him I'd probably drop bookings by ten percent."

"How did he take that?" Jessica asked with a grin. She liked the way Cat handled her boss.

"Pretty well, actually. We understand each other most of the time. I told him if the budget's tightening up then we need more money for marketing, to get more bookings. But no, he has an MBA so he knows my job better than I do," Cat frowned ferociously. "The man's an egotistical son-of-a-bitch sometimes."

"Don't badmouth bitches," Jessica said. "Some of my best friends are bitches."

Cat laughed. "Okay, I'll just say he's an asshole."

"That's better. By the way, I'm going to be in a showcase there next week."

"Really? Showcase? Must be the speaker's association."

"Yep. I volunteered for it for the local contacts. I don't think I'd really mind at all if I had more engagements locally. Pays less, but local events aren't quite so wearing."

"I wonder how you do it," Cat said, shaking her head. "I enjoy traveling, but you're off two or three times a month. I don't think I'd like that."

"I'd really like to have more of a pattern to my life. I —" Jessica wanted desperately to say she had given up her traveling ways and Cat could count on her to be around. "I like my new home and I want to stay there more."

"Well, it certainly is dull when you're not around," Cat said.

Jessica's heart leaped and she leaned toward Cat. Cat suddenly smiled like a child on Christmas. "Oh goodie, the show's starting. Let's get these opening acts out of the way. I can't wait for Steve Martin. I saw him two years ago at the Boardinghouse."

Jessica completely ignored the first performer because she was wondering if Cat was hinting . . . maybe unconsciously saying . . . sort of subtly admitting to some feelings for Jessica. Fool, Herself pronounced. She's a little lonely after Paul. There's no more to it than that!

She heard Cat hiss. Cat looked angry.

"Oh, come on girls," the performer on stage said. "Have a sense of humor." There were more hisses.

"What is it with women these days? You gotta give 'em a financial statement before they'll go out with you, take out a loan for the date and whad do ya get," he appealed.

"What you deserve," Cat said darkly. Several people at tables around them snickered.

"Ya get chewed out for not bringing protection along," the performer continued. There were a few sparse laughs among more hisses. He finally retired amid some polite clapping and not so polite boos.

The next act was a vast improvement. Jessica had heard some of the jokes before, but the short fat comic had a wonderful firecracker delivery. His repertoire included famous TV theme songs played on the paper bag.

"God, he was good," Cat gasped as they applauded for him. "After that male chauvinist pig, I was prepared for the worst."

"I didn't know you were such a feminist," Jessica teased.

"I'm not — I mean I am. I wish it weren't a dirty word these days."

"Why do you say that?"

"I don't know. I used to really believe in feminism. I still do as a principle. But somewhere along the way, I got bored. It was the same old thing, the same old complaints. I felt as if nobody was doing anything, just sitting around complaining. So I cancelled my subscription to *Ms.* and just went about my business."

"I think I know what you mean. I fell out of the movement, too, mostly because I stopped feeling connected to it, represented by it. I've been feeling bad lately, letting other people do all the work."

"How so?"

Someone nearby hissed for them to shut up.

"Hey, this guy's good," Steve Martin announced about himself, strumming his banjo.

Jessica had to admit he was.

Cat leaned across the table. "Didn't I tell you he was funny? Wasn't I right?"

"Yes, yes you were." Jessica took a deep breath to relieve the pressure on her sides.

As they were walking home, Cat picked up the threads of their earlier conversation. "You said other people were doing all the work. What work?" she asked.

"Equal rights for everyone," Jessica said slowly. She decided to take a chance an bring up gay rights. "I'm a real fan of Harvey Milk's."

"I do admire him," Cat said slowly. "I'm not sure I believe in everything he stands for, but sometimes when he's speaking he reminds me of Bobby Kennedy. I was only a girl when he died, but I remember thinking he was so handsome and exciting. When I see him on film now I get cold shivers and I wonder what the world would be like if he'd lived."

"I get the same feelings sometimes," Jessica admitted. "I feel depressed. But now there's something I can believe in, letting people live their own lives. I know I should do something."

"I gave money to a couple of campaigns, but there hasn't really been anything, or anyone, I believed in that much." Cat sighed.

Jessica desperately wanted to talk about subjects which might get an opinion on homosexuality out of Cat. She still didn't have the courage to say, Look, I'm a lesbian, I hope you don't mind. If you mind I'll die, but don't let that worry you.

"I remember how I felt when I first saw Gloria Steinem," Cat volunteered. "I'd been oblivious to the way the world was changing around me. She turned my world over. One day I was worrying about my nails and the next I was a card-carrying women's libber." Cat hung her head, as if she was admitting to some heinous crime.

Jessica smiled in the darkness. "My mom and dad died when I was nineteen. I didn't have anyone else to rely on. I was absorbed in studying for a while, but I don't think I'd have survived college if it hadn't been for the support I got from the women's center. What happened to me?"

"What do you mean what happened to you?" Cat demanded indignantly. "You're a wonderful role model. You teach women how to be smart in the business world and how to get their objectives met, overcome resistance."

"It's not enough. I even make a point in one of my lectures about everyone having to pay rent for their time on earth with some meaningful purpose. What's my purpose? Just making speeches and consulting?"

"What more is there?"

"I don't know. I don't feel very strong, but I should be able to do more. I've toned down my ideals over the years and did make it to the mainstream of the speaker's circuit. Maybe I should get back to the fringe so I can speak my mind."

"I think I'd like to be there when that happens," Cat said seriously.

"When I get ready to break out, you'll be the first to know, I promise," Jessica said, equally seriously.

They stared at each other for two or three of Jessica's tense heartbeats, then Cat grinned. "How'd we get so serious after such a funny show? Come on, I think there's a great science fiction B-movie on."

"A what movie?"

"A very bad science fiction movie. They're great!"

"Bad, but great?"

"Sure, like *Invasion of the Bee Girls. The Navy versus the Night Monster.* Godzilla movies, you know, the classics."

"Oh. I gather I've missed something." Jessica was almost relieved that they had steered away from more tense subjects. Go slowly, Jessica, Herself warned. Go slowly.

They began watching a perfectly awful movie called *The Last Dinosaur.* Cat gaily pointed out the flaws in the geological time frame.

"They have human-like creatures co-existing with dinosaurs. At that point, the only mammals around were little tiny mole type animals. And look at the sexism. The airhead photographer drops her purse and the apemen don't want it, but an apewoman keeps it. Really!"

"And why is the black guy carrying a spear? Do any of the white guys carry spears?" Jessica demanded. She was trying to get into the spirit of the movie.

"It would appear not," Cat said sadly. "Stupid, sexist *and* bigoted. This one's too bad for me. I don't think there's anything else on. Oh well." She turned off the TV. "There really are movies that are bad but not so insulting. Like Godzilla movies. Just silly."

"I don't believe I've ever seen a Godzilla movie."

"Well, I just happen to have the original *Godzilla* on videotape. This VCR was a complete extravagance but it's great to have my favorite movies on tape. *Godzilla.* And *Attack of the 50 Foot Woman.*"

"How convenient," Jessica hedged.

"You think it's silly," Cat said accusingly.

"Well," Jessica said slowly, "it feels good to be silly. Let's watch *Godzilla.*"

"Silliness suits you," Cat said. Jessica looked over at her and studied the line of Cat's profile as she watched the movie. What had that remark meant? Anything? Was she just hoping for feelings that weren't there?

Questions, questions, Herself moaned. When are you going to get some answers?

* * * * *

"For my presentation, I'll need a volunteer. You'll have to put up with criticism and a lot of teasing," Jessica announced. There didn't seem to be a lot of eagerness in the crowd.

"I'm game," said a familiar voice, and she turned to find Cat coming up the steps to the stage.

She'd seen Cat once or twice during the course of the showcase. Now Jessica tried to control a blush as she considered her task.

"Image. Would anyone in the audience care to guess what this woman does for a living?" There were a few random guesses. "I heard middle management, banking, and sales."

She gestured to Cat. "Let's take a look. Bright blue suit, pearl pink blouse, an unusual necklace. I'd definitely say not IBM, or banking. Middle management, perhaps. Sales is probably a good guess. But did anybody notice how quickly other jobs were ruled out? Nobody guessed she was a clerk, or a bank teller. Nobody thought she was an engineer, or a computer programmer. Nobody guessed she was a librarian or a nurse. On the other hand, nobody guessed she was a chief executive officer. Why? Can it be that on very little evidence we make snap judgments about people?"

Jessica said to Cat, "Assuage our curiosity and tell us what you do."

Cat leaned toward the microphone. "I'm the sales manager here at the Regency."

"How many people report to you?"

"Seventeen."

"And your annual budget?"

"Including salaries and marketing, over two million." There were a couple of gasps in the audience.'

"And your name?"

"Catherine Merrill."

"My first suggestion to you, Catherine —" It felt odd to call Cat that "— would be to change your explanation of what you do. Next time you're asked, try saying, 'I'm the sales manager at the Regency. That includes supervising seventeen people and managing a budget of over two million dollars.' Think of it as your chance to sell yourself. Now people know your title, and they have an idea of how much power comes with it."

Jessica went on, going over Cat inch by inch, from her neat professional hairstyle to the tips of her navy blue pumps. As she went, she illustrated the major points of her self-image seminar. Cat took it all very well. She walked back and forth and answered questions, and seemed to be enjoying the experience. Jessica's twenty-five minute spot was over very quickly and the response overall was enthusiastic.

She went out in the hallway with Cat, laughing gaily. Inside she was exhausted with the horrible strain of looking at Cat, noting every inch of her, from the earrings glistening in the beautifully-shaped earlobes, to the pale hose clinging to well-shaped legs. She wanted to tell Cat how much she adored every inch, every last inch of her.

"That was fun," Cat said, "and you're certainly good. It was easy to answer your questions, but if I'd had to just talk in front of all those people I would have choked."

"I like public speaking, but I get stage fright all the time," Jessica said brightly. I want to kiss her, I want to hold her. I want to be silly and mushy.

A harried looking woman emerged from a service corridor. "Ms. Merrill, that woman from the dentists is having a fit over the lunch room set-up."

"Didn't she talk to banquet?"

"She says she won't deal with anyone but you."

"Holy merde!" Cat exploded. Then she smiled and shook her head. "I'm sorry, Elaine, I didn't mean to yell at you. Thanks for finding me. Gotta go, Jessica, it was fun."

"See you later," Jessica said, waving the suddenly alien Cat away. She was used to Cat's jeans and T-shirts and casual way of taking life. This efficient-looking woman with the brisk air was rather foreign and frightening. And adorable just the same, Herself said.

Oh shut up, she said to Herself irritably as she collected her case and thanked the planner for inviting her to speak.

Oh Cat, Herself sighed. So near and yet so far.

Skip the bad poetry, Jessica told Herself quite firmly. Let's go home and read some Elizabeth Barrett Browning. We might as well do this mooning about thing properly.

EIGHT
The City That Never Sleeps

"Bring your tray-tables to their full and upright locked positions."

Jessica put her book down and put her tray-table up. Next to her Cat was dozing and at Jessica's touch she started up and fastened her seatbelt.

"That nap did wonders for me," she said. "I'm ready for this town."

"I still don't understand why you had to be the floor manager last night."

"Because the GM couldn't care less about my plans. He enjoys making everyone's life miserable. It's the way he's built."

"Sounds like a sadist."

"He is. But he pays well."

Soon they were in a cab heading for the heart of Manhattan.

"I wish the driver spoke English," Cat said to Jessica, under her breath.

"He understood Regency and I think that's all that matters." The driver glanced over his shoulder and smiled broadly at them and they smiled back, glanced at each other and suppressed their nervous giggles.

The time was late for New York, but barely after nine p.m. San Francisco time when they checked in. They borrowed an iron and ironing board from housekeeping and spent the rest of the evening unpacking. They would be there for eight days. As Jessica lay still that night, listening to Cat's steady breathing, she wondered if it was just her imagination that the room was getting smaller already.

The shared airplane ride had been a dream come true. She had been able to watch Cat sleep. She worried about the way she was mooning over Cat. It wasn't healthy and it wasn't going anywhere. She was barely functioning most of the time. And every moment was precious. She wanted to save up a lot of them for the time when Cat would go out of her life.

The next day, Sunday, they started out by hiring a horse-drawn carriage for a ride through Central Park. The trees were gold and green and auburn. The air was cool and crisp and smelled of smoke fire. Jessica sat back and watched Cat play with her

111

camera. The cab driver dropped them at the far side of the park on Fifth Avenue and they went over to Madison and took a bus uptown to the Guggenheim. They started at the top of the spiral like everyone else, strolling along and looking at each painting. Initially their different views on the arts didn't conflict too much, until they came to a group of cubists.

"I can't find the Nude," Jessica said.

"On the staircase, don't look at it literally.

"I can't find the staircase," Jessica said stubbornly. Actually, she appreciated Duchamp but it was fun to tease Cat.

"It's a step outside the traditional art. It was breaking down the old barriers, allowing for more freedom of expression. Cubism was the end of the way it used to be," Cat explained, her voice getting brisk.

"What about modernism? What about DeKooning and Pollack? What about them?"

"You faker." Cat slapped Jessica's arm playfully. "You do appreciate modern art."

"I appreciate it. I don't necessarily care for it. There is a difference."

"Yes, there is. I appreciate Bach but I don't necessarily care for him. But that doesn't mean I'd shoot somebody for listening to him."

"Ah," Jessica murmured, "appreciation and tolerance. I wish there were more of it."

Cat looked at Jessica oddly and only nodded. They continued down the spiral, arguing over which movements had meant more, and whether Diego Rivera was a part of the Ash Can School. Cat said yes. Jessica said no.

112

A guide interrupted their good natured arguing, handing them a catalog. The young woman smiled at Cat and said, "I'm sorry, but Diego Rivera painted in the thirties and forties, long after the Ash Can School. He deserves a school of his own, really, but you may place him with Thomas Hart Benton if you want to remember his time period." She turned to Jessica. "I hope you had money on it," she said with a toothy smile. There was a teasing light in her eyes.

"No, I didn't, but thanks anyway," Jessica said, smiling back at the guide. Cat frowned, but conceded she might have him confused with someone else.

Jessica continued to chat with the guide while Cat wandered on to the next few paintings. There was something in the woman's eyes, the way she used her hands that told Jessica she was gay, and that she was interested.

The possibility of sharing a few pleasant hours with this woman just didn't matter, not anymore. She wanted Cat and only Cat, and she wasn't fit for anyone else. On another trip, maybe a year earlier and she might have pursued a liaison. Eventually she said "Nice to meet you," and joined Cat. There was only a tiny whisper of regret from Herself, and it was all from her libido.

"My feet are killing me," Cat said a few hours later. They were in Bloomingdale's and loaded down with several bags. "Let's get something to eat and rest up for the walk back to the hotel."

"How about we get something to eat and rest up for getting a *cab* back to the hotel?" Jessica suggested.

"That sounds even better."

They wandered into a deli and got a couple of sodas and lox and bagels. "Jessica," Cat said suddenly, "do you mind if I ask you a personal question?"

"I never mind the asking, it's the answering," Jessica answered with a smile, and her heart began pounding. She prepared to say yes quite simply, yes, she was a lesbian.

"Have you ever thought about having a child?"

Jessica blinked. "No, I mean, yes, I have. I haven't ever done anything about it. Can I ask you a personal question?"

"Sure."

"Why do you ask?"

"Because I've been wondering," Cat said slowly. "I'm thirty-two. I don't have any particular guy in sight I think I might marry. Sometimes I wonder if I ever will. But I'd like to have a child, spend a part of my life raising a girl, maybe. Adoption's pretty hard to do, and expensive."

"So you're thinking about getting pregnant?" Jessica asked. She told Herself Cat would make a wonderful mother.

"I've been thinking maybe that's why I believed Paul when he said he'd changed. I didn't really care if he had or not — I was subconsciously trying to get pregnant. I tried so hard to make it work with him . . . I faked a lot of things." Cat smiled a little sideways. "Especially to myself, but it wasn't great. It wouldn't be like when — well, if he and I went to a movie and one of us didn't like it, we'd fight. It wouldn't be fun, not like when I go to the movies with you. I was depressed a lot. Oh, I don't know. I'm sorry I brought it up. It seems rather morbid to

114

be talking about Paul and biological clocks in the most spectacular city in the world."

"Most spectacular city on the eastern seaboard, if you please," Jessica said teasingly, lightly. Her pulse was racing and there seemed to be a sudden shortage of oxygen. Cat had just said she found Jessica more fun at the movies than Paul. Would she someday make the next leap and realize Jessica might be more fun in bed? "I like San Francisco," she went on. "And talking about having a baby isn't morbid. Just think about the idea very carefully first, think about your finances particularly."

"I have. I can't possibly afford a baby — the time away from work, the extra insurance, the responsibility, the stress. Forget I brought it up. Can I ask you another personal question?"

"Okay."

"How'd you get so experienced? You have good advice on almost every topic."

"My mom always said I was born forty years old. I don't know, common sense mostly. I try to think matters through by balancing logic and emotion."

"Lucky you, you can keep your emotions under control." Cat sighed. "I've only learned to do it because of a series of bad mistakes where I didn't stop to think before I did something emotional."

"I don't have a perfect record," Jessica said softly. I screwed myself up by falling for you, she wanted to say as Cat raised her eyebrows. "My heart has gotten me in trouble. I'll tell you about it sometime when I'm too drunk to think better of it."

"Deal. Ready for more shopping or go back to the hotel?"

Jessica stood up and bounced experimentally on her toes. "There's enough bounce left in me for one more floor at Bloomingdale's."

The floor of their choice was the lingerie floor. Cat confided that silky, slinky lingerie was a major vice of hers. "I glide around my place, the queen of all I survey. I think I'd be shocked for someone to actually see me in some of them."

"I think I know what you mean," Jessica managed to say, fighting a blush as she pictured Cat in the pale rose negligee Cat was considering.

"I'd have to get the boudoir slippers too. Nope, I can't afford it. Let's get out of here before I decide I can." They got on the nearest escalator and headed for the street. "Saved in the nick of time," Cat laughed. "My American Express card is already just about worn out."

"Oh, darn it all," Jessica exclaimed. "Here, sit down and wait for me. I think I set my sunglasses down on one of the displays. I'll be right back." She hurried off before Cat could decide to come with her.

When she returned there was another bag Cat couldn't see tucked inside of the Big Brown Bag she was carrying. It's a birthday present, she told Herself, a Christmas present. Never mind that it's not exactly the thing one woman gives another as a gift. Never mind that before she wrapped it she would hold it to her face and imagine it caressing Cat's body.

She lay awake again that night, listening to Cat breathe and Herself began to worry. Look, you've got to stop this. This is silly. You just can't go around like a love-sick dog for the rest of your life. Tell her how you feel and take the consequences.

But she'll never speak to me again, she said to Herself, and I'll never see her again. We won't even be friends because she'll be afraid I'll jump her every time she comes inside the door.

Which would be just as well, Herself said back. Then you could get on with your life. For chrissakes, you've wasted the whole summer, not to mention some very wonderful opportunities for some very choice sex. The woman in the museum, for example.

What about the woman in the museum?

You were attracted to her, she was attracted to you and you could have had a very nice time.

Sex isn't everything.

Herself laughed uproariously. You're a basket case, Jessica. You haven't even prepared for the lecture tomorrow. You're just going to use the same old material and hope no one has seen you before, as if that were possible on this circuit. There's nothing new about you, Jessica. You're hopeless. She isn't good for you.

But I've never been in love before. It's something I want to do.

So cross it off your list and get on with your life. Herself pouted and refused to discuss the matter further so she went to sleep.

* * * * *

Cat was up first and out the door to catch a train to the Long Island Regency where the first day's lectures and tours would be held. Jessica wasn't speaking until ten so she took her time, arriving around nine to survey the audience and get a feel for the audience.

117

A clothing consultant was first up and Jessica didn't envy her one bit. She was getting every argument Jessica had ever heard about why women shouldn't conform to male business standards. She wanted to explain for the thousandth time that male didn't automatically mean bad. It might mean stupid, it might mean dull and conservative, but not necessarily bad. But she wasn't on the podium, some other unlucky woman was.

"It's up to you," the speaker said. "But you need to be aware of the consequences of dressing in a way that your bosses, the people who set your salary, might think means you don't belong. You might be the one in a thousand who can wear anything and command respect. The rest of us have enough battles to fight without worrying about our clothes getting us into trouble."

"But isn't it up to women to make things change and not just act like men?" another asked. Jessica cringed at the heavy layer of makeup and the low-cut blouse. That woman would go through life wondering why men saw her not as a professional but as a sex object.

Her turn to speak came soon enough. The topic was very narrow — how to handle on-the-job harassment and survive. Her speech went very well and she was satisfied with her presentation.

She went to the hotel's coffee shop for lunch and was invited to join a group of women from the morning session. They were very flattering and Jessica felt her ego getting all shiny. So what if she was a total emotional mess. At least she still had pizzazz.

The afternoon passed quickly as she sat in on other sessions. After the last session she went up to her room. As she stepped out of the elevators and headed down her wing, another woman and a bellman came out of a room. Jessica stopped short in startled recognition.

"Marilyn!"

"Jessica, what on earth! How long have you been here?"

"Since Saturday night. You're leaving?"

"Yes, but I can trim it about fifteen minutes. I'll get my bags downstairs," she told the bellman and she and Jessica went back into Marilyn's room.

Marilyn pulled her into her arms and Jessica felt her senses melting. It had been a long time since she'd been kissed like this — the last time had been with Marilyn, in fact.

She closed her eyes and felt a delirium sweeping over her. Marilyn caressed her through her jacket and skirt, then her jacket slid to the floor and teeth nibbled through the thin material of her silk blouse.

Jessica clung to the shoulders now pressing against her thighs, trying to maintain her balance. Hands swept up under her skirt, caressing her through her nylons. Lips pressed against her stomach and she felt their fever through her clothes.

She ran her fingers through the thick hair, breathing rapidly, breathing hard, lost in sensation.

"Oh — oh Cat," she whispered.

Marilyn went rigid. Jessica opened her eyes, expecting Cat to be kneeling in front of her. She gasped.

"Oh God, Marilyn, I'm sorry. I'm so sorry."

119

Marilyn got up and walked to the other end of the room. Jessica reached out for her, tears in her eyes. She let her arms fall back to her side.

"I'm so sorry."

"So who is this Cat person?"

"My neighbor."

"Convenient."

"No, not really."

Marilyn turned to look at her and then dropped her gaze. "I'm the one who should be sorry. After last time we'd pretty much decided we wouldn't do it again, didn't we? And you know what, I've been mentally and physically faithful to Sherry since then."

"The woman in Corpus Christi?"

"Yeah. But seeing you again —" Marilyn put her hands over her face, then drew a deep breath. "I shouldn't have touched you. It undid me."

"I'm sorry," she said again.

"So is this Cat the woman of your dreams?"

Jessica nodded and she couldn't stop her tears. "I really love her."

Marilyn's expression softened. "Sorry I was a bitch. You're not happy are you?" Jessica shook her head. "She's with someone else?" Jessica shook her head again. "She doesn't like you?"

"She likes me a lot, I think. She's straight. I watch her go on dates and we decided it would be fun to go to New York together instead of going alone and I listen to her breathe. . . ."

"Poor, poor baby," Marilyn murmured, and she came back to put her arms comfortingly around Jessica. "Poor, poor little one. I am sorry. What are you going to do?"

120

"I don't know. I keep asking myself that and I just don't know. I love being with her. I thought I could get by with just a little part of her life, but it's not working out. I think I'm going to lose her."

"If your life blows up and you need a change of scene for awhile, you can come to San Antonio. One of our living suites is yours. No strings. You can just be alone. Or bring your word processor if you want."

Jessica looked up at Marilyn and then kissed her gently. "You are a good friend, for an ex-lover."

"I try." They smiled at each other, not very happily, and Marilyn picked up her room key. "I really have to go."

"I know. Let's keep in touch this time, okay? I miss your phone calls."

"I'll call, I promise."

At the elevator they shook hands. As the doors closed Jessica realized she hadn't even asked Marilyn if she'd secured the capital for the New York hotel. Feeling selfish and self-centered, she went to her room, hoping Cat wasn't there. She wanted to change and repair the damage Marilyn had wrought to her poise.

* * * * *

The week passed quickly. On Friday afternoon her conference wrapped up. She was the last speaker, giving her estimation of where women were heading in the business world.

She scanned the audience as she spoke, keeping eye contact with the key faces she had chosen to gauge reaction. When she saw Cat standing at the back, she didn't miss a beat or stumble over a single syllable. She suddenly felt right about the change she was going to make to her usual "stick with it and we'll get there" speech. It wasn't in the same league as an I have a dream speech, but she felt a new edge of steel in her voice when she began her closing.

"I feel good about where we've been and where we've come, but I want to leave you with a word to think about. Complacency. We see more of us earning more money, and yet women make up the poorest segment of our population. We see more of us in management, and yet we're clustered into pink collar jobs where the salaries just happen to be two-thirds of the salaries in other areas.

"Complacency. I've been complacent for the last few years. It has brought me considerable security and financial well-being. But for the last few years I haven't really slept well. I've been nervous, wondering if my security was just a sham. I've been wondering if I began reminding women about the fact that we babies haven't come a very long way would I lose some of my security? Probably.

"And as I've finally realized what toeing the line means, treasuring my security over my ideals, I've felt deeply sorry for the men who've toed the line all their lives. We can be freer than they were. Through our freedom we can make men free too. Our daughters and sons will be freer still. That's what in the women's movement for all of us, a new world with more choices. The businesswoman is a woman. Her needs are remarkably similar to the needs of all women.

"Give me what I need and I'll give you what you need. Give me what I'm worth and I'll give you my loyalty. Give me respect and I'll fight anyone who would take yours away. Let me fulfill my dreams, and I will amaze you with my strength! Thank you for listening."

She swept off the podium to shake hands with some of the women in the front row, so invigorated she didn't hear the applause.

"You're really dynamic on the podium," Cat said when Jessica was finally finished with the circle of women who had come up to her.

"Thank you. I'll trust your judgement and agree. But I heard one person saying, 'Oh dear, she's getting political.' "

"Screw 'em," Cat said with the toss of her head that Jessica found excruciatingly adorable. "You made me uncomfortable. I had to wonder what price I paid for my job security. I tell myself no one's outright sexist anymore, but a part of me knows my boss gives me the worst schedules, the toughest standards."

"Don't quit your job on account of what I said. I hope I didn't leave that impression. Push for change. Every little inch you gain will mean a mile for the next woman." They walked to the elevators. "What's on for tonight?" Jessica asked.

"Someone told me there's a dance bar called the Jukebox around here somewhere and they play prime music from the fifties and sixties — no disco merde! I said I'd meet some of the other reps after theater time tonight, but I don't have to go. It was a loose arrangement."

"Sounds fun. Where do you want to have dinner?"

"Tell the truth, I'd love room service. I'm glad everything's over and I want to relax."

"That's the best suggestion I've heard so far." She was feeling good, brave. Maybe tonight, Jessica thought. I want to tell her how I feel. I can be brave. I made the speech today and survived, maybe now's the time.

She ordered their dinner while Cat changed into some jeans and a pullover. She had to turn and stare out the window while Cat changed. It was too hard to watch.

Lust, she decided, was a bitch.

They decided to stay comfortable in their jeans and pullovers and went to the play that way, their clothing mingling with the multitude of styles of the rest of the audience.

"What a thriller," Jessica said afterward. "I was on the edge of my seat the whole time!"

"I wasn't too sure about something called *Deathtrap*, but it was terrific," Cat admitted. "When the two guys kissed and I realized they'd set the whole murder up — it was great!"

"That's what I call a good play," Jessica said. "Do you want to go meet those people at that dance place?"

"Yeah, why not? Let's go dance till we drop."

Jessica fell suddenly silent in the cab, vividly remembering the last time she'd gone dancing. It had been in New York, the night she'd met Gina. No, there was no going down that road again, she told Herself. There is just Cat now.

"Earth to Jessica. We're here," Cat said, giving her a puzzled look.

She followed Cat into the bar. "There they are," Cat pointed and they made their way to the rowdy group in the corner.

124

They were fun people, Jessica found, a little more boisterous than she was used to, but what the hell. She danced with all the men and watched Cat dancing too. Cat was graceful and animated — she moved well.

Jessica wondered if she had the same look on her face all the men who were watching Cat had on their faces. Probably, she thought. Her partner swung her gently to "Fooled Around and Fell in Love." She sung along with the words, smiling secretly. Her partner asked what was so funny. "Nothing, nothing," she said. Cat's going to catch you with your tongue hanging out like the rest of them, Herself warned.

The place closed at three with everyone singing "American Pie," singing about the day the music died. The critical moment had come, Jessica realized. Cat had spent the last little while in deep conversation with one guy who was the same physical type as Paul the Jerk. When they hadn't been talking, they'd been dancing. He kept putting his arm around Cat and Jessica had to guard against glaring at him.

She, on the other hand, had spent most of the night talking to several different women about their careers and sharing war stories. She'd danced with the men and they'd talked a little, but when they found out what she did for a living they'd obviously figured she wasn't worth the challenge. That's the way it always was. She was glad men were so predictable because it saved a lot of awkwardness.

As people headed for the door to catch cabs, she wondered if she should let someone else drop her off, or if she should ask Cat if she was ready to go back to the hotel. She was almost sick inside. Would Cat go off with the Paul the Jerk clone?

"Jess, do you want us to drop you at your hotel on our way?" someone asked, and she glanced over her shoulder at Cat.

Jessica was flooded with relief as Cat disentangled herself from the clone. She smiled very nicely and then told a big lie about having just enough time to pack and catch a flight back home.

"Yes, we'll just make it," Jessica added, glancing at her watch.

She saw Cat relax. Everyone shook hands all round amid promises to keep in touch. She and Cat caught a cab.

"Thanks for the quick save," Cat said on the way back to the hotel. "He was going to take no very badly. I kept trying to wiggle out from under his arm, but he was sure I was completely besotted."

"No problem. It's a shame you just can't say no politely and that's the end of it."

"Not with his type. I'm worth more than two drinks and a couple of dances."

"I'll say."

"Thanks," Cat said, grinning. "How much do you think?"

"At least three drinks," Jessica said. She wished she could expect to buy Cat three drinks and take her to bed. And she wanted so much more than that.

"Poor guy, if he'd only known."

Jessica shrugged. "He's one of those men who treat women like slot machines. Put in a few quarters and you might get lucky," Jessica said, resting her head back on the seat. She blushed. And was glad

126

Cat couldn't see her. Hypocrite, Herself called her. Isn't that exactly what you've done all along?

The hotel lobby was very quiet but the Bee Gees were pulsing from the hotel disco.

"How about a nightcap?" Cat suggested and Jessica nodded.

She expected the bar to be packed, with John Travolta imitators dancing up a storm. But there were only a few couples in the place and the bartender perked up a little at the prospect of having someone to serve.

By leaning very close to each other they could converse if they screamed over the loud monotonous beat. It was a relief when the music segued to the gentler *How Deep Is Your Love*. Jessica found her lips getting a little closer to Cat's ear each time she leaned toward her. She slid a little closer to Cat until her knee was against Cat's.

Jessica was not aware of what they talked about. She was only aware of how close Cat was to her, how much she wanted to lean just a little further and brush her lips over the softness of Cat's neck, let kisses wander down the neckline of Cat's soft sweater, let her senses take in Cat's smell and taste.

Cat seemed to notice nothing. After they finished their drinks they wandered up to the room. For a long time Cat stood at the window, only turning away from the glistening nightline as Jessica pulled the covers up to go to sleep.

"What a city," Cat said as she went to the closet to get her nightgown.

"I think it actually does sleep."

"Only a little. But there's this feeling that anything could be possible." Jessica gulped. Cat turned out the light and went into the bathroom with a quiet, "Good night, Jessica."

"Good night." She was beset with regret. The magic moment to tell Cat how she felt had come in the hotel disco — they had been so close — but Cat couldn't have heard her over the music. Maybe tomorrow. After all, anything was possible in New York. Cat had said so.

NINE
Fever

They didn't get up until lunch. They decided to see more museums and then stand in line at the half-price booth to see what was available in the way of a play. Jessica felt groggy from her poor night's sleep, and a little hungover, though she didn't remember drinking enough to justify having a hangover. She wanted to make her declaration, but she had a terrible headache. And she kept right on treasuring Cat's every move, adoring Cat's every word.

"This will take all afternoon," Cat said as they surveyed the line.

"Why don't we go to a comedy club instead," Jessica suggested. She didn't feel like standing in a long line in the bright sun.

Cat thought for a moment then agreed. "There's the Improv. Let's call when we get back to the hotel to see if we can get in."

"Look out!" Jessica yelped, pulling Cat's arm so she wouldn't try to cross the street where dozens of cabs were fighting to the death. Cat stumbled and for the briefest moment Jessica felt the full pressure of Cat's body against hers. It made her weak and breathless and warm all over.

Unblinkingly, Cat looked at Jessica for a few moments, then pulled slowly away. "Let's go to the top of the Empire State Building," she suggested, turning away.

"Where is it?" Jessica fumbled with the guide book, hoping her color wasn't as high as it felt.

"Fifth Avenue, somewhere around thirty-third. A couple of blocks from here."

The New York afternoon was relatively clear. The air was cool, but Jessica was finding the sun oppressively hot. Her skin felt as if she were getting a sunburn. She wandered around the observation floor of the Empire State Building while Cat broke out her special filters and wide-angle lens.

"I might need more film," she said when Jessica joined up with her again.

"It's about ten dollars a roll at the gift shop.

Film is more expensive than the Statue of Liberty spoon," Jessica told her.

"In that case," Cat said, "I'm through with the pictures. You seen enough?"

"Yeah." Jessica had felt reasonably poised until she'd seen Cat concentrating in her single-minded way on taking pictures. Now she felt as if she was walking around on pavement that was a hundred degrees; the air seemed to move in the illusory waves of sweltering heat. She was hot and sticky under her sweater.

The elevator was crowded and seemed even hotter to Jessica. Is this what swooning is all about, she asked Herself.

"Are you all right, Jessica?" Cat asked.

Her voice seemed very far away. "I think I need to sit down," Jessica whispered.

Cat put her arm around Jessica's shoulders and she went weak in the knees. She wanted to throw her arms around Cat, hold her and be held until the world was right again — at least until it was cooler. She sat down on a bench.

"What is it, Jessica, what can I do?" Cat's voice was gentle and concerned. "Would you like something cold to drink?" She started to rise.

"No! No, just stay here with me." She felt as if she were burning up. Her mind wasn't functioning right. The ground seemed to waver and the air was oppressive.

"We're going back to the hotel," Cat said firmly. Jessica was aware of voices and then Cat was helping her to stand. Then they were in a cab working its way back to their hotel.

Once in the room Cat left Jessica on the bed while she got some ice. Jessica was desolate and her breath started coming in tiny, half-crying gasps. A cold cloth came out of nowhere and soothed some of the pain in her head.

"You're burning up," Cat said, but Jessica didn't hear her. There was pounding in her ears and the room was taking on psychedelic colors. She felt hands on her body and she tried to ward them off. Her own hands were captured and held. She focused on Cat, who was stroking her head.

"Lie still, shhh, just lie still. Everything's going to be all right. I want to make you more comfortable. Lie still," Cat whispered. Jessica closed her eyes and went limp.

She moved again only when a T-shirt was slipped over her head and again when Cat pulled fresh underwear onto her.

There were voices and comings and goings but she ignored them all. She was only restless when the hand holding hers went away. She found that if she whispered, "Cat," the hand came back. It was the only solid and real thing in her nightmarish world.

She lost track of time. The room was light then dark then light, and in one of the darknesses she stirred and became aware of another body not far away from her, breathing quietly.

It was so very hard to open her eyes and turn her head. At last she managed to move and there was Cat's face not far from hers, looking pale and tired, showing lines of stress Jessica had never seen before.

"Cat," she said softly. She wanted to caress the beautiful face lightly but her arm didn't obey her.

Then Cat's eyes flew open in alarm as Jessica said her name again.

"Jessica," Cat whispered back and then she sat up, moving carefully. She laid a cool hand on Jessica's forehead and nodded. "Your fever's gone." Jessica closed her eyes and after a moment the hand moved down her face to caress her cheek.

"Hey, don't go back to sleep. I want you to drink some water," Cat said softly and she shook Jessica just a little.

Cat got up and went to the bathroom. In the dim light Jessica saw Cat come back with a glass, watched her sit down on the edge of the bed. She pulled Jessica into a sitting position, cradling her in her arms. But instead of taking the glass, Jessica slid her arms around Cat. She felt Cat shiver and their embrace tightened. For a moment, Jessica felt they were connected, inseparable.

"What's wrong with me?" she asked at last and Cat released her and held out the glass.

"Drink first." She waited until Jessica had taken a few swallows. "You've had the measles, lord knows where you got them. I've already had them."

"Measles," Jessica echoed as she handed the glass back. She rested again on Cat, her head comfortably cushioned by a soft shoulder and the curve of a soft breast. After a few minutes Cat laid her back down and covered her up. Jessica held out her hand and Cat took it, sitting down on the chair next to the bed.

"You held my hand while I was sick, didn't you?" she asked dreamily. Cat's hand felt very comforting and permanent.

"Some of the time. You calmed down that way." There was a long silence before Jessica spoke again.

"What day is it?"

"Tuesday."

"Our flight?"

"Left without us this morning. It's okay, we're booked for Thursday," Cat assured her. "You'll get well fast, don't worry. The doctor was sure you'd be fine."

"The doctor?"

"I got scared and called for one."

"I'm sorry —"

"It's not your fault. The doctor was more concerned about the consequences if you were pregnant. I told him I didn't think you were, but he said there's always a chance."

"No, there's no chance at all that I'm pregnant," Jessica whispered and she began to slip into beckoning sleep.

"Go to sleep," Cat whispered softly.

"Ummm," Jessica nodded as she drifted off.

* * * * *

Daylight streamed into the room and she sat up slowly. Cat was sound asleep in the other bed. By persevering, Jessica was able to stand up and find her way into the bathroom.

She wasn't prepared. Her eyes seemed to be her only living feature, huge and burning in her splotchy face. She sat down on the john as her legs started to wobble, fumbling in the mess of cosmetics for her toothbrush. She knew she'd feel better if she could only brush her teeth.

She had to stand again to rinse out her mouth and she did feel almost human. Her hair was disgusting, matted and oily. It would only take five minutes to shower. She could stand up for that long.

She lasted only two minutes, just long enough to strip, adjust the water and lather up her hair. Then her arms wouldn't cooperate, her legs trembled, and although she didn't want to, she was suddenly sitting in the tub, water running over her, and with no way to get up and out. Feebly she tried to rinse her hair, but a flutter of panic built in her. Will I drown if I pass out, she wondered.

"Oh God, Cat, help," she murmured, and the shower curtain was pulled back abruptly.

"What the hell are you doing?" Cat said harshly. "Get out of there!"

"I can't," Jessica whimpered and Cat's angry expression faded, but only a little.

"I have never seen such a fool," Cat muttered and she bent to lift Jessica to her feet. She got in the shower with Jessica, the spray plastering her cotton nightgown to her body.

"I am a fool, Cat, an utter fool," Jessica said forlornly, then she spluttered as water and shampoo ran over her face.

Cat helped her get the shampoo rinsed out and then sat her down on the john to be toweled off. Jessica couldn't stop a trail of weak tears from running down her cheeks.

"Oh merde, stop crying," Cat ordered, but Jessica only sniffed and shook harder.

After drying her off, Cat stripped and then dried herself. She brought a clean T-shirt for Jessica. "Come on, into bed with you."

"I just wanted to be clean. I felt so awful." Jessica leaned on Cat's naked body. Until now, she had perceived Cat as soft and gentle. Now Cat felt tough, strong enough for her to lean on.

"I know, just lie down," Cat said, much more gently. "You scared me again, and I don't like it. No more scaring me, that's an order."

"I promise," Jessica said and then she blew her nose loudly and faded back onto the pillows Cat had plumped up.

"Your vacation was ruined," Jessica said after a while.

"So was yours," Cat responded, stretching. She got dressed, shrugging into a pair of jeans and a sweater. The soft, clinging sweater made Jessica want to stroke Cat as if she really were a cat — all soft and fluffy. But Cat wasn't soft and fluffy anymore. She was an Amazon, Jessica decided. A very short Amazon.

"I'm sorry," Jessica murmured. A faint daze was taking over her, a glow of exhausted happiness. Cat cared about her.

"It's not your fault. Look, I'm going for a walk to get some energy back. If you get out of that bed, so help me I'll spank you."

After Cat left she watched the news. The upcoming elections and whether balance in the House of Representatives would shift was the top story along with speculation about who would succeed John Paul I.

She squeezed her hand, remembering how it had felt when Cat held it. She decided she had two choices. One: move and get Cat out of her mind and heart. Two: tell Cat how she felt, then move and get

Cat out of her mind and heart. It was a depressing choice, all the more because she really didn't want to move again. But she knew she'd never get over Cat if she saw her every day.

And why would an Amazon like Cat want to even be neighbors with a silly weakling like you, Herself demanded. Measles, indeed. She was helpless to stop Herself from asking all sorts of unpleasant questions.

What had happened to the woman who never let her heart (or other influential parts of the body) rule her head? When had she turned into such a puddle of jello, Herself wanted to know.

When had she last had sex? When would hotels stop bolting lamps to the tables? She giggled at Herself. Obviously, Cat had driven her insane with lust and she wasn't to be held accountable for the fact that her mind had stopped working. I get to be crazy, she decided.

She felt a lot better. I'll just tell her I'm nuts, that I'm in love with her and it's all her fault.

She practiced. "I'm madly in love with you, I want to make love to you, I'm crazy about you and I'm deranged and it's your fault." It sounded so good she went to sleep, rehearsing her little speech, over and over.

TEN
Truth and Consequences

The flight home was horrible. Jessica's entire body ached. Even Cat's sweetness and gentleness didn't make her feel better. She tried not to complain or cry, but somewhere near Denver she couldn't stop a trickle of tears.

Cat put her arm around Jessica and wiped her face. "We'll be there soon," she whispered over and over and Jessica turned her face to Cat's softness and tried to control her tears.

"You're an Amazon," she mumbled, her eyelids drooping. It was the highest compliment she could think of at the moment. Her lips were operating independently and as she dropped into sleep she was sure Cat hadn't heard her over the drone of the plane. She wasn't even sure she had spoken aloud.

* * * * *

It was days before she was back on her feet. Cat continually checked on her, brought her food, insisted on taking her out for some light exercise. She had to cancel two speaking engagements and set back her final report to the software company by a month. She had a lot of time on her hands and nothing to do but study the election races.

About a week after they returned Cat came home from work with pictures from the trip.

"I haven't even looked at them," she said.

"These are really nice," Jessica said from the sofa. Cat brought her a glass of cold water and went back into the kitchen. Slowly Jessica went through the photos, remembering the fun they'd had together — until she had gotten sick. She remembered how close she had been to telling Cat everything.

She began a now stack. The top picture was of herself. It was the first on the roll, and Cat must have been fiddling with her camera and snapped it not intending to keep it. At any rate, Jessica hadn't been ready for the picture — her expression was far too revealing.

She was leaning against a wall, evidently assured that Cat wasn't looking at her. She cringed as she studied the photo, not believing she could have such

139

a dopey look of adoration on her face. Anyone who saw this picture would know she was mooning after the person she was looking at. If Cat saw it, she would know Jessica was looking at her.

Jessica stuffed the picture under the sofa cushion just as Cat came back into the room. She desperately hoped there weren't any more candid shots of her in the rest of the prints.

Life fell into a regular pattern. Cat fixed Jessica dinner every night, convinced she would starve otherwise. Jessica went on with her research as soon as she could concentrate, although Cat scolded her for not resting enough. She convinced Cat that her word processor wasn't making her tired, it was keeping her interested by playing games with her. Cat did not like computers.

"I'm getting better," Jessica protested one evening. "You shouldn't be fussing like this. You look awfully tired."

"Thanks, I feel like a million bucks," Cat said brusquely, then she smiled, but it faded into a sigh. "Sorry. Guess I am tired."

"Cat, I really do appreciate your being here," Jessica began. She wanted to be strong again, not such a noodle of need and weakness before she told Cat her feelings. "But you aren't responsible for me, really. I don't want you to get sick." She smiled broadly. "I don't think I can be such a good nurse."

"You're an easy patient. Maybe I should have been a nurse and not a businesswoman."

140

"How are things at the hotel?" Jessica asked to change the subject.

Cat sank down into the cushions and took a long drink from her soda and then sighed. "Effective last Monday I have a new boss. Mark resigned while I was gone and he left almost immediately for another job. The new guy is a crony of someone from Corporate."

"So what's he like?" And why didn't you tell me sooner, Jessica wanted to ask. She felt a little hurt, but she supposed Cat hadn't wanted to worry her. Besides, what's it to you, Herself commented.

"He's pure ice. I can't decide if I don't like him because I was never given an opportunity to apply for his job, or if he's just unlikable. I think I could do his job, but he does have a degree in marketing, and that precious MBA."

"Ever thought of getting an MBA yourself?"

"All the time. I can't go any further without it. But I'm not convinced I want to go further. I keep thinking about a baby."

"Choices, choices." Jessica sighed. "Why are women's lives so filled with choices? Directions that seem irreconcilable. You can have one, but not the other."

"You said you had a choice to make, remember, a couple of months ago. Do you mind my asking what you decided?"

Jessica captured Cat's gaze and held it. "You can always ask me anything," she said, staring into the gleaming brown eyes. "I know what I want to do but I'm not ready to begin. Part of the solution is returning to my ideals." Cat blinked and the electric contact between them lessened, but didn't completely dissolve. Jessica could still sense the beat of Cat's heart, the rate of her breathing. "I was a feminist — you know, that dirty word — when I was in college. When I graduated and began moving around to take temporary consulting assignments I lost track of my friends and who I really was. I guess I kind of sealed myself up."

"It's a big transition from college to working. I know what you mean," Cat said. She leaned back, completely relaxed.

Jessica went on. "It's been ten years. And ever since I moved here, I don't know why, maybe it's because this place has so much light in it, anyway, I've really seen myself in a different way. I want to be freer."

"You strike me as pretty free," Cat said, wiggling her toes.

"Well, have you ever heard of the Johari Window?"

"No — maybe. It's a communication theory, right?" Cat ventured, her head to one side.

"Right." Jessica wanted to give her a kiss for a reward. "The window has four parts, remember? Take me, for example. There's what you know about me that I don't know."

"That would be like if you had spinach stuck to your front teeth, right?"

"That's it. There's what you and I both know, like the fact that my eyes are blue. There's what neither of us knows. My instructor called those the great mysteries. Her example was when she and her husband were in a car accident and she ripped the door off the car to get him out. Neither of them knew she was capable of doing that."

"The great mysteries. It sounds like there's so much to be discovered in each person." Cat stretched and then curled up in the corner of the sofa.

Dragging her gaze from Cat's expressive face, Jessica went on. "She characterized the mysteries as probably the most joyous area to explore. The last area is what I know about myself that you don't know. Those are the secrets." She chose her next words carefully. "I've never forgotten what she said. That the larger the area of secrets is, the less free you are. You become circumscribed by the fear of someone discovering your secrets. For a lot of women, it's fear that their feminism, their fundamental belief that women are free, equal and just maybe superior in many ways to men, will be discovered and men will make reprisals."

"I think I see what you mean. But if you have no secrets —"

"Then you are completely free. And you have to take the consequences of having no secrets."

"Like admitting to someone you'd had a mental breakdown," Cat suggested. "People will treat you differently and you have to be strong enough to handle that."

"I think I'm strong enough. So I'm just waiting until the right time to start getting rid of my secrets," Jessica said. She closed her eyes and feigned a nonchalance she certainly didn't feel. "So I've changed my speeches a little, my outlook a little. I'm trying to be less worried about how I might lose an assignment and more concerned with motivating women to get rid of their secrets. We'll all be freer."

Cat sat up and turned on her side to face Jessica. "You've motivated me," she said with a flash of a brilliant grateful smile that dazzled Jessica. "I'll tell you my current secret, it's got me kind of worried and I just thought I'd keep it to myself. I glossed over my new boss because I didn't know quite how to say it. Maybe it's my imagination, but he's been complimenting me a lot, not just on my department or my numbers, but me."

"Uh-oh."

"Yeah, uh-oh. I have an extremely firm policy about mixing business and pleasure. I did it once and got burned so bad I'll never do it again. But that's beside the point anyway. I'm *not* attracted to him," Cat said firmly. "And he's married. But he keeps saying things like how much he likes the suit I'm wearing, what good taste I have, all in a very icy but direct way."

"Icy doesn't fit with a come on," Jessica said.

"I mean there's no feeling in it. He's cold when he says it, not flirtatious. But for example this morning, he said, and this is a direct quote, I've never had the pleasure of working with a woman so admirable in every way. Flat out, no inflections, no significant eye contact."

"How does he treat other people?"

"I guess the same way, I don't know. He makes me uncomfortable. What am I supposed to say to that?"

Jessica thought about it. "That's a tough question. If it's the way he treats everybody, you can probably relax. But if you think he's singling you out, I'd be careful about any extracurricular activities, including going to lunch or dinner."

"Am I wrong to be so suspicious?"

"No, not at all!" Jessica leaned over to pat Cat's

arm and she gave it a comforting squeeze. "Call it woman's intuition or gut instinct, but something in you is saying uh-oh. Your instincts are right most of the time."

"I feel better," Cat said. "I feel better just having talked about it." She took Jessica's hand and held it.

Jessica felt a shiver run over her shoulders and little twinges of desire swirled over her body and settled excruciatingly in her nipples.

Cat looked at her in concern. "Are you cold? Do you feel a chill?"

"No, no, really. Just someone walking over my grave," Jessica said.

Cat smiled. "Considering how sick you were, I'm not so sure that's a wise expression to use."

A silence fell between them and Cat let go of Jessica's hand. Maybe I'll never wash it again, Jessica told Herself. Herself told her not to be silly.

"I want to be silly," she said.

"What?"

"I'm sorry," Jessica said. "I was just thinking out loud." Whoops! She's turned your whole life upside down and around; you don't even know what you're saying anymore, Herself said. What a wonderful and frightening thing, to be remade like this, she thought. I feel young and foolish, and she makes me feel vibrant and wise.

Excuse me, but I'm going to throw up, Herself announced.

"Hey, where'd you go?"

"Sorry," Jessica mumbled.

"You really are one to go off. They must be very deep thoughts."

"Where no man has gone before," Jessica said and then laughed.

"Oh, that reminds me *Star Trek* is on," Cat said. She grabbed Jessica's remote and turned on the TV, switching channels. "Ah, this is a good one, 'Balance of Terror.'"

They watched in companionable silence, Cat tucking Jessica up again. She had never had time to watch much TV and somehow she had missed out on *Star Trek*. She'd see it once or twice, but had never been a fan.

"We are much alike, you and I. In another reality I might have called you friend," Cat quoted softly along with the Romulan commander before he blew up his ship. "Isn't that a wonderful idea?"

Jessica was touched a little, too, but embarrassed to show it. It was just a TV show, after all. "Male bonding," she observed quietly.

"What do you expect for 'sixty-eight? I'm the first to admit there are few meaningful women characters in *Star Trek*. But the idea that different races and beings could live side by side in peace was rather novel at the time. It still is."

"You got that right. Tolerance and acceptance." Jessica remembered using those words in New York. Cat seemed to remember too because she nodded. There was a long silence. "Hey," she finally said. "I'm not the only one who gets lost in thought around here it seems."

"Sorry. What do you want for dinner?"

"I'm not really hungry."

"Tough," Cat said briskly. "You have to eat. What'll it be?"

146

"How about some of your stew from yesterday and a roll?"

"And a glass of wine?"

"Sure."

Cat went into the kitchen. Jessica leaned back and shut her eyes, soaking in the complete domesticity of the situation. From the time Cat got home from work until she thought Jessica should go to bed, she stayed at Jessica's. She looked in on her way to work, usually bringing her some breakfast. Jessica knew she didn't need cosseting anymore, but she didn't want Cat to stop.

Little things, like Cat holding her hand, made her wonder if Cat was attracted to her and not aware of it. She wanted to take a chance and let Cat's feelings grow. And when the time was right, please make it soon, she'd tell Cat how she felt and hope she didn't scare Cat away with the intensity of her love. She wanted to propose a marriage to Cat, a partnership meant for eternity.

"You want butter on your roll?" Cat called.

"Yes, sure, and some Parmesan cheese."

"Okey dokey. Is there anything else on TV?"

"I'll check." While she'd been daydreaming, *Charlie's Angels* had come on. Neither she nor Cat could stand to watch the jiggling. "There's absolutely nothing. Some stupid movie of the week. Why don't we listen to some music?"

"You mean like Bach or something?"

"You got something against Bach?"

"Not really. I'm actually getting to like him," Cat admitted from the kitchen. "You seem addicted."

"Can't help it. Consider it a vice."

"Oh, so another dark secret is revealed. I thought

your only vice was fine wine, ma'am," Cat said as she carried in a tray.

"I lied." Jessica dug into her stew. "This is even better than yesterday," she said genuinely.

"Thanks. Don't change the subject. So you lied about vices."

"And are you vice free, ma'am?" Jessica asked.

"Nope. Don't say I am, neither."

"So what are your vices?"

Cat giggled and took a deep breath. "Chocolate, Italian food, lingerie, sleeping late, trashy romance novels, doing nothing for long periods of time, long lunches, bad science fiction movies and used record stores. And I like to watch *The Incredible Hulk*. That's all I can think of right now."

"Impressive list," Jessica said. "I suppose I'll admit to a vice for chocolate and Italian food, and used record stores, too. But you can keep the romance novels." At least the heterosexual romance novels, Herself added.

"How about the bad science fiction?" Cat asked.

Jessica looked down, and picked at a piece of imaginary lint. "I have a confession to make," she whispered, rather sullenly. "I watched *Ghidrah the Three Headed Monster* today, and . . . I liked it," she said in a rush, hiding her face in pretended shame.

Cat laughed delightedly and threw her arms around Jessica for a quick hug. "I knew it," she exulted. "You have trashy impulses!"

"I guess I do," Jessica admitted. More than you know, she added to Herself. Your mind's in the gutter again, Herself noted. I like the gutter, she answered testily.

"What other trashy impulses do you have?" Cat pressed, grinning. "Come on, 'fess up, now."

"I — I like Merv Griffin."

"No!"

"Yes," Jessica insisted and Cat laughed gaily.

"That's too much. Hey, another Godzilla movie is on this Saturday. We should watch it together with the appropriate amount of popcorn."

"I didn't think I'd enjoy Godzilla so much," Jessica said sheepishly.

"So let's watch Godzilla sightsee Tokyo next Saturday."

"It's a date," Jessica said.

Cat began collecting the dishes and Jessica felt her words hanging in the air, even though Cat seemed to notice nothing. It was a kind of date. Maybe she'd bring flowers, maybe she'd begin to subtly court Cat.

But she didn't want to seduce her, overwhelm her. If she were a man, she wouldn't have to worry about making sure Cat was comfortable with the idea of loving her. If she pushed Cat along and they became lovers, Cat might wake up someday and tell her it had just been an interlude. She had to make sure Cat loved her, and accepted their relationship for what it would be: a lesbian relationship. That, after all, was why she'd never had a successful relationship. Maybe she and Marilyn could have been lovers if she had ever admitted they were lesbians. She smiled. That was behind her. She had never felt so good about who she was and what she was doing with her life.

She also knew she'd never felt so miserable and horny and tenuous, as if she were standing on the edge of a precipice. She'd either jump into the abyss or fall into Cat's arms.

They watched *Charlie's Angels* and bet on the plot. It seemed obvious to Jessica how the entire episode was going to run so she risked a Snickers bar.

"Jill will be in a car chase and the sleazeball will break down and admit he murdered all the stewardesses," Cat predicted.

"Kelly will be in the car chase and the sleazeball will break down and admit he murdered all the stewardesses," Jessica predicted. She was wrong. Jill was in the car chase; it was high drama.

"Okay, okay. I don't have a Snickers bar at the moment. But as soon as I do I'll pay you off," she promised.

"I'll charge interest," Cat threatened. "A Reese's Peanut Butter Cup for every day you're late."

"That's highway robbery!"

"Take it or leave it," Cat insisted, grinning.

"Okay, okay. Shylock," she accused.

"Welcher."

"Salesperson!"

"Consultant!"

"Well!" Jessica feigned great insult and swatted Cat. "I never!"

"It shows — isn't that the classic comeback?" Cat hopped up. "I've got some contracts to go over so I guess I'll go home. Promise me you'll go to bed by eleven. You think you're stronger, but you still look awfully pale."

"This is San Francisco. Everyone is pale in San Francisco."

"Not as pale as you are, silly," Cat said gently. "Promise me," she coaxed.

"Okay, Mommy. I'll go to bed at eleven," Jessica said. I'll read until I want to go to sleep, she thought.

"Good. Nighty-night."

* * * * *

She had nothing to wear. She was going to Cat's to watch the Godzilla movie and there was nothing to wear. She wanted to look pretty. She wanted Cat to notice her. She wanted Cat to be subtly aware of her body.

Jeans obviously were a must. Cat had introduced them into her life and she would wear them to honor her. Besides, they were comfortable. She remembered the 'Women Do It Better' T-shirt and put it on, tucking it into her jeans. And sighed. She looked like a stick. A particularly uninteresting stick in a cardigan. Her eyes were blue, but they weren't a very remarkable blue. Not like Elizabeth Taylor's. Her hair was so ordinary she hardly noticed it. Curly and brown, easy to take care of, but maybe she should consider something more dramatic, something less complacently professional. Using bobby pins, she pulled the sides back and flat so the top was still curly. Her face looked more square, but she looked overall less staid. Next week she'd get it cut differently.

Glancing at the clock, she dashed into the kitchen for the chilled pouilly-fuissé and the bundle of white roses. Tonight was a date of a sort, and she owed Cat so much — much more than just helping her when she was sick. She owed Cat for jeans, and T-shirts, and trashy science fiction movies. And for love and hope. She prayed that someday she could tell Cat just how much she owed her.

"Roses! Jessica, you shouldn't have," Cat protested, but her expression told Jessica that she loved roses.

"They're a thank you. You've been more than a friend over the last few weeks."

"It was easy to do. Well, my goodness. Thank you. And you brought my favorite wine, too." Cat led the way to the kitchen and clambered up onto the counter to find her best vase.

"Don't drop it and cut yourself," Jessica warned.

Cat laughed. "No, you filled the year's quota for that." She arranged the roses in the vase. "Tell me what you had to eat today."

Jessica recounted her menu, delighting in Cat's continuing concern. Cat had stopped fixing dinner every night, at Jessica's insistence, but she still wanted to know what Jessica ate.

"You need more leafy greens," Cat observed. "I like your hair, by the way."

"Thanks. I'm thinking of getting it cut." Don't blush, whatever you do, she told Herself.

"It would look good. Two minutes to Godzilla and counting. Let's pour some wine."

They each curled up in a corner of the couch with a bowl of popcorn between them. As the movie began, the phone rang.

"Merde! It never fails." Jessica turned the volume down while Cat answered the phone. "Hello? Oh. Hello, Jim." Jessica froze. Jim was Cat's new boss.

"What a shame. Oh. I thought my synopsis was very clear. Oh well, fire away. That complicated? No, now really isn't a good time, how about first thing Monday morning? I'm sorry, I'd forgotten about that. Well, sometime tomorrow, I could meet you at the hotel. Oh. Yes, I do understand how important the contract is. Of course. Of course. Very well." Cat's eyes were wide with dismay.

"Do you need my address? You have my file. Well, I'll see you in just a little bit." Cat hung up, and ran a slightly shaking hand through her hair. "What am I going to do, Jessica?"

"What did he say?"

"He's leaving for a corporate meeting tomorrow afternoon. He was going over material on a major contract for the meeting and has some questions too complex to discuss over the phone. He's on his way."

"You didn't tell me he'd been more persistent," Jessica said, anguished at Cat's quandary.

"He hasn't. A group of us went to lunch yesterday and he sat down the table, away from me. I didn't like the way he was watching me but I never thought he'd do this, call me at home. What am I going to do?"

"Well, I won't leave. Tell him I'm your roommate."

"He probably knows I live alone. Everyone knows that at work."

Jessica took a deep breath. She lectured on harassment and what was needed right now was a calm, objective approach. Inside, she was livid. Objectivity was hard when someone she loved was involved. "You shouldn't have to worry about how much your boss does or doesn't know about your

153

personal life. He shouldn't be coming over at nine o'clock on a Saturday night. I won't leave. I'll play very obtuse and just sit here. If he's on the level, I won't bother him one bit. We'll tell him my place is being fumigated and I have nowhere else to go."

"But you won't always be here, Jessica. What if he makes a pass and when I turn him down he fires me?"

"Then you sue his ass!" she said hotly. Then she calmed down. She wasn't going to help Cat by getting more upset. "If he's unpleasant tonight, you start a log of everything he says to you, how he addresses you differently from everyone else. Listen to me. I lecture on harassment, Cat. You can protect yourself. If you have to leave your job, then they owe you."

"I can find another job," Cat said, "I can. Maybe I should."

"Listen to me," Jessica said again. "I'm here. Don't run from him. If you do, he wins. And he gets to put the make on some other woman." She took Cat by the shoulders and gave her a little shake, like a trainer sending a prize fighter out into the ring. "You're strong and you can make things better for other women, especially those who can't find other jobs as readily, who can't risk being without a job for even two weeks."

Cat blinked and put her arms around Jessica, hugging her tightly. "Thank you. You're so strong. You make me feel like I can do anything."

Jessica tried not to go rigid. She tried to feel natural as she put her arms around Cat. It took great effort to not stroke the smooth back or the soft hair. She hugged Cat briskly instead and then pushed her away.

"I happen to think you're pretty strong, lady. You're stronger than some guy with overactive hormones and a power complex."

Cat smiled a little wanly and took a deep breath. "Let's hide the wine. I don't want to have to offer him any."

"Good. Stick to soda or coffee, and only if he asks. You're not entertaining him. And Cat —" She hesitated until Cat looked at her. "I won't leave. I don't care what he says, I won't leave."

"Thanks."

When the bell rang Cat answered the door promptly, opening it wide, smiling graciously. "I think it's terrible for you to have to work so late, especially when your wife must be missing you on a Saturday night."

Good, Cat, Jessica thought, you let him know you know he's married.

"Well, this contract is very important —" He broke off when he saw Jessica.

"Jim, this is Jessica Brian. Jessica, this is Jim Barton, our director of sales and marketing."

"How do you do," Jessica said guilelessly. The man had the eyes and the handshake of a fish. A dead fish.

"A pleasure to meet you," he said. There was an awkward silence. Jessica was distinctly aware that Jim was waiting for her to leave.

"We can spread the papers out on the table, Jim," Cat said, moving her centerpiece out of the way.

"Uh, this contract is very hush-hush," Jim said, looking at Jessica.

"Oh, don't mind me. I'm not in the hotel business. I'll just go back to watching the movie."

155

She plopped back down on the sofa and nibbled popcorn, even though she thought she would choke.

He said something in a low voice to Cat.

"Jessica's apartment is being fumigated so she's staying with me until she can go back," Cat said in a clear voice. "Let's get to work, shall we? It's already so late."

Jessica knew absolutely nothing about hotel management, but she knew enough about contracts to find his questions very stupid. Cat was careful, briskly professional, and meticulous in answering his questions. He stayed only thirty minutes, the last five spent slowly putting papers away, joking about people in the office.

"Well," he said, "I thank you for being available to answer these questions. I'm glad I didn't interrupt anything important."

It was all Jessica could do to keep from snorting. Men were so stupid! Conversations between women were never important to them. If only they knew — perhaps it was better they didn't.

"I'll try to get my summaries to you sooner," Cat answered quietly, "so we don't have to do this again. Have a good trip." She closed the door.

Neither of them said anything until they heard the elevator cage doors open and close. Then Cat exhaled. "It's not my imagination, is it?"

"No, I don't think so," Jessica said. "I think you need that glass of wine now."

ELEVEN
What's Past Is Prologue

Each day Cat grew more jumpy. She would tell Jessica about interaction with Jim Barton and Jessica would boil the details down to factual statements they recorded. Looking at the printed words seemed to help Cat calm down and stop blaming herself for what was happening to her. Jessica hardly remembered her life before she met Cat, and now her day revolved around when Cat arrived home from work.

"We got a big contract today," Cat began slowly one chilly November evening. "It arrived all signed and I of course reported it to him in the due course of activities. He . . . he hugged, all friendly like, but his hands were under my jacket, around my waist. I couldn't help myself, I pulled away." She stopped talking, and coughed. "I told him I didn't think it set a good example for my subordinates."

"And what did he say to that?" Jessica didn't meet Cat's eyes, partly to give Cat some privacy while she talked, partly because her own glittered with anger.

"He said What's a little hug between friends? I told him I tried to keep things very professional with my staff and I would appreciate it if he would help me uphold that image."

"Excellent," Jessica said warmly. She squeezed Cat's hand. "You're on record now."

Cat stood up abruptly and paced the living room. "But it didn't do any good. Before he went back to the office, he patted me, right here." Cat rubbed the small of her back.

"Have you seen him touch anyone else like that?"

"No. Never. I've watched."

"Has anyone seen him touch you?"

"The department secretary, a few other people. I want to quit," Cat said all in a rush, with another cough. "I'm going to get my resumé out to the other hotels in the City. I don't have to take this."

"No, you sure as hell don't. But you don't have to leave, either."

"I've thought about it for a long time. I can't sleep at night, so I worry about what to do."

Lack of sleep accounted for the pale face and red eyes, Jessica decided.

"When I leave, I'll write a letter to the board of directors and to the general manager stating my reasons for leaving."

"But what about the other women in your department?"

"I heard through the grapevine that he left Dallas because of an unpleasant situation with a secretary. With my excellent record they might just believe me when I tell them why I'm leaving. I might keep him from getting promoted anywhere else, and have him watched. I don't want to go to court." Cat coughed again.

"I don't blame you. Even though a part of me thinks you should press your case and get him fired. If you change jobs for less money, you should be compensated. But I understand. Harassment cases take four to six years to settle because it's a whole new body of law." Jessica couldn't contain her concern and outrage any more. "But it just isn't fair to you!"

Cat went on pacing. "I know. But I want to put this behind me. I can't stand going to work anymore. I used to like my job and the people there."

"I do understand, Cat, I do," Jessica said intensely. Cat stopped to stare out the window and Jessica stood behind her, noting the line of Cat's face profiled against the stars. "It's as if you're being assaulted, every single day."

Cat turned in shock. "I don't want to think about it like that!"

"But how else can you think about it? He's

forcing you to submit to his will by shutting off your options," Jessica snapped. "I'm sorry, Cat. I'm not mad at you. I want to push him out a window." She reached for Cat, to hold her, to smooth the lines in her face away.

Cat stepped back. "I don't want you to think I'm a moral coward. I'm not, but I just don't have the energy to fight him and the entire corporation."

"You can do one thing to help your conscience," Jessica said, swallowing her hurt feelings. She had been forward to reach for Cat like that. "In your letter, state you'll cooperate with any internal inquiry if circumstances permit. It will be up to them, and they can't say you didn't give them a chance to rectify the situation."

"Okay. That sounds workable. Will you help me write the letter when the time comes?" Cat paused to cough and went on. "I can use your advice."

"Sure. I don't mean to push you. I hate to see you unhappy." Cat smiled wanly. "Are you coming down with a cold?" she asked.

"I don't think so, but I've had this cough all week."

"It might be stress," Jessica suggested.

"Probably," Cat agreed glumly. "I have a stack of contracts to go over, so I guess I'll go home. See you later." And she was gone.

Jessica changed into her fuzzy green robe, her favorite robe of all which she had unearthed for the cold San Francisco nights. It was luxury to lie on the sofa in her fuzzy green robe, reading poetry and sipping jasmine tea. Her mind would have been easier if she could have stopped worrying about Cat — but she did relax a little.

160

Never in her life had she wanted to protect someone so much. Never had she felt this way. I feel as if I'm dying, Herself said sadly. Unbidden, a quote came to her mind. She flipped forward a few pages and found the words in her anthology.

"Guess now who holds thee / Death, I said. But there the silver answer rang / not death, but love," Jessica read aloud. "I'm not half dead, I'm just half alive." The book slid through her fingers and she stared at the ceiling.

She had a choice. She could stop sitting around and mooning. All she needed to do was get up off her duff and get out into the network.

You know the network's there, Herself said. Take advantage of it.

Not yet, not quite yet.

What are you waiting for?

I don't know. Something to happen.

It's pointless.

Go away.

Herself sulked.

I like my body when it is with your body, she whispered in her mind. *Muscles better and nerves more,* she continued, her eyes closing. She could almost feel the silkiness of Cat's hair, the smoothness of her skin. She drifted, imagining, fantasizing.

* * * * *

Jessica was in the midst of typing in a lengthy citation for her book when the phone rang. Wearily, she marked her place. The phone had been ringing continuously since lunch.

"Jessica, it's Cat. I really need your help!"

"Anything, Cat, what's wrong?" She heard the near hysteria in Cat's voice.

"Jim asked me to go out tonight. He has these play tickets. I lied and said I had a prior commitment and he really pressed me about breaking it. He said we should get to know each other better, especially since he thinks I might be up for a promotion to another property — and he wants to be able to say he really knows me. Oh, Jessica —" Cat broke off.

"It's okay, go on."

"Well, I really dug myself into a hole," she said shakily. "I told him you were dropping by to pick me up for a meeting at a women's association, that you'd be making a speech and I'd be making a presentation on our hotel and you were not in your office so there was no way to call it off. It was so lame, but it was all I could think of. And I thought he'd be leaving around four-thirty but I just heard he's sticking around until six tonight. I said you'd be here at five."

"It's okay, I can make it. Really," Jessica said, trying to give Cat an infusion of calm energy. "I'll be there a little early, in my best bib and tucker. I'll look at my watch a lot and ask to borrow your phone to call and confirm my speaking time. Did you say where the meeting's at?"

"Sausalito, seven o'clock. That's why we need to leave at five," Cat said, in a low voice. "I can't believe I panicked like that. But I was so scared —"

"It's okay. I'll be there before you know it."

"Thanks, Jessica," Cat said. "I really owe you."

"I'll think of an appropriate payment," Jessica said, in a teasing voice. Like maybe you could love me for the rest of your life?

162

She put on her don't-screw-with-me white silk blouse and navy blue pinstripe suit. Jim Barton had better not mess with me, she thought grimly.

She found the sales office by 4:55 and asked for Cat. Cat appeared almost immediately.

"Jessica! I'm almost ready," she said loudly, with a big smile.

Jessica responded in kind, feeling as if she were in a play. She knew Cat too well to be fooled by her smile. The lines around her eyes were filled with tension.

"We can't afford to be late," she said as they walked back to Cat's office. Cat gathered up her briefcase and purse, and an armful of hotel brochures. Jessica saw her tense as Jim Barton walked into the room.

"Off to your meeting?" he asked lightly.

"Yes. Jim, you remember Jessica Brian, don't you?"

"Sure do, I never forget a face," he said, shaking Jessica's hand.

He sure does remember you, Herself commented wryly. You're the bitch who screwed up his first pass at Cat. Jessica smiled vivaciously. "We're going to risk the Sausalito ferry," she said.

"Marin County Businesswomen's Association," she said.

"Some women's meeting, right?" he said.

"Must be a big slice of business for you to give up an evening," he said to Cat.

"They're thinking about doing an exhibition. Of course, I think they should hold it here," Cat said, smiling. Jessica thought her smile was so brittle it might break.

"Isn't that Katy's area of responsibility?" he asked, playing with his tie and unbuttoning his grey suit jacket.

"Usually, of course. When they mentioned their idea at a meeting, Jessica promoted me as the person to know, so I couldn't very well pass the presentation onto someone else after the big build-up Jessica gave me. I'm very interested in their Association, too."

And what the hell difference is it to you, Jessica wanted to demand. Why do you care how she spends her time off?

"Well, I hope we get a contract out of it," Jim said pleasantly. "Your department could use the numbers."

Jessica got mad. She knew Cat had an above average rental rate, the best of all the Regencys in California. She tried to keep a handle on her temper as Cat began to edge toward the door of her office.

"We do try," Cat said, smiling, smiling.

"I know you do, kid," Jim said, and he put his arm around Cat, squeezing her chummily. As Cat walked toward her door his hand went to the small of her back, patting Cat as if she were some pet animal.

Jessica saw red. How dare he touch Cat! As she turned, she saw a small table with glasses and a full pitcher of ice water on it. Her action was spontaneous and well-choreographed.

"Cat, aren't you forgetting your brochures?" Jessica asked, and she turned back toward Cat's desk. Her briefcase swung out and rocked the little table. The pitcher toppled and spilled its contents on what was closest to it — which just happened to be Jim.

The water and ice cubes splashed onto Jim's

crotch, then down the entire front of his grey pants, leaving a dark wet trail. Jim shouted and grabbed at the pitcher. The rest of the water poured onto his shoes.

"Oh, I'm so sorry! How clumsy of me," Jessica protested. She grabbed a couple of Kleenexes from the box on Cat's desk, then bent to dab at Jim's soaked kneecaps. "Oh dear, these aren't really going to help." She batted her eyelashes just as Marilyn did when she was playing innocent.

"I'll call housekeeping to come and mop up the water," Cat said, going back to her desk. She turned her back on Jim and Jessica, but not before Jessica saw her shoulders quiver with barely restrained laughter.

"I'm just so sorry. I just can't believe I did that," Jessica said again.

"It's quite all right," Jim said.

Jessica could tell it wasn't quite all right. What's the matter, loverboy, she thought, did your ardor get dampened? Herself went off into gales of laughter, but Jessica kept her expression guileless.

"You must send me the dry cleaning bill, you simply must," Jessica said.

"Oh no, it's just water. I'll go and find a towel," Jim said and he quickly disappeared down the hallway holding his jacket closed over the very obvious watermark on his pants.

"Let's go, shall we?" Cat said in a bland voice.

"Oh let's," Jessica agreed, equally blandly.

Once in the elevator, Cat began to laugh. She laughed all the way out to the street.

Jessica pulled her into a doorway, out of sight

165

from the hotel. "Stop laughing, Cat," she ordered. Cat's eyes were filling with tears.

"It's too funny. The look on his face," she gasped out.

Jessica fumbled in her purse and found a tissue. "Come on, take some deep breaths. Blow your nose and let's get out of here," she said, glancing over her shoulder. "You don't want him to find you having hysterics."

"Thanks, Jessica. I feel so much better. Maybe he'll just decide I'm bad news and leave me alone," Cat said hopefully. "He deserved to get water all over himself. I'm so glad it happened."

"You don't think it was an accident, do you?" Jessica asked.

"Well, of course — no! Jessica, you didn't."

Slowly, Jessica nodded, a tiny smile playing about her lips.

"You wonderful, wonderful woman." Cat threw one arm around Jessica's shoulder as they walked, giving her a quick hug.

"Yes, I know. I'm pretty wonderful. Want to buy me a pizza?" Jessica's heart was pounding from Cat's nearness.

"I'll buy you two pizzas! Can we change first?"

"Sure. Jeans and sweatshirts?" Jessica asked.

"Would I wear anything else?"

"I wonder what Jim's wearing right now," Jessica mused.

Cat started to laugh again. "He lives in Walnut Creek. He has an hour's commute."

"With wet pants on. Gee, I guess he'll be a little embarrassed." Jessica giggled. "The devil made me do it."

166

"I like your devil," Cat said. "Do you have any other wonderful qualities I don't know about?"

Jessica choked on a swallow and was speechless all the way home.

* * * * *

"I wish I could get a decent night's sleep," Cat said the following Sunday night. She had been pacing for almost an hour. Jessica felt as if she were watching a volcano walk back and forth in her living room. "I'm running on adrenaline and caffeine right now. I don't know how you stand me."

"I understand why. You're not bothering me at all, please believe that," Jessica said firmly. "Let me help."

Cat stopped pacing and looked toward Jessica, but she still had a faraway look. " 'City on the Edge of Forever.' "

"Say what?"

"A great *Star Trek* episode. Let me help is a more powerful phrase than I love you, according to one Captain James T. Kirk."

"Oh." Perhaps that was right, Jessica considered.

"I was able to duck the dinner invitation for last night, but I'm running out of excuses. I can't pour ice down the man's pants every time he gets out of line," Cat said with a weak smile.

"I wish you could," Jessica said darkly. "It's too good for him. Castration's a thought."

"You're so bad, Jessica," Cat said with a half-hearted laugh.

Jessica realized that she was not being very successful at cheering Cat up. Jim had intensified his proposals for dates and dinner and Cat was to the point of confrontation — and probable unemployment.

"I wonder if I'll ever sleep again," Cat observed a few minutes later.

Jessica considered the pale face, puffy eyes, the nervous cough, the hair that didn't seem to glisten anymore. A plan formed in her mind. "Let Aunt Jessica take care of that," she said with a bright smile. She selected two albums from her collection and went to the door. "Come on, we'll see if my magic system works for you."

Cat smiled brightly, too, and Jessica sensed the effort it cost her. "What are we going to do?"

"Don't you worry about a thing. You're not to think about anything, okay? Run along and change into your pajamas," she said as they went to Cat's apartment. In the kitchen, she poured them both a glass of milk. She put an album on the player and turned the stereo up.

"Now what?" Cat said from the doorway. She was wearing a nightshirt with New York Cat emblazoned across it.

Jessica thought she was adorable, but found it easy enough to forget she was burning with fever for Cat, at least for the moment. She had to help Cat get some sleep. "Into bed with you," she ordered and she followed Cat into her bedroom. Like a little girl, Cat clambered into her bed, fluffing up her pillows, sinking down under the covers.

Jessica put the album on and drew up a chair, dimming the light in Cat's bedroom just a little. "Have some milk," she offered and she kicked off her shoes and curled up in the chair.

The narrator on the record began and Cat gave a

squeal of delight. "Peter and the Wolf! I haven't heard this in ages. The french horns are the wolf."

"Right you are. I like Leonard Bernstein's voice, don't you?"

"Shhh," Cat ordered imperiously. "I want to hear."

"Okay, okay," Jessica said, smiling.

"The oboes? The duck! Of course, I just forgot. The flute I know is the bird. And the clarinet is the cat, yes, I know that. I've always thought of myself as a clarinet."

Jessica didn't agree. She thought Cat was a cello because a cello affected her the way Cat did. They both made her heart soar. Whenever she listened to solo cello she wanted to cry. She rested her head on her knees and watched Cat enjoying the story.

"Uh-oh, the bird and the duck don't see the sneaky old cat coming," Cat said, her eyes beginning to droop. She snuggled down into the pillows, wiggled her feet and finished off her milk.

Jessica smiled gently to Herself.

Well, Herself observed. You certainly are in a bad way.

I know. I think she's started to need me, to want me to be there for her.

Don't you want her to need you?

Yes. But I want more. I want her to feel needed and loved. I want her to feel desire for me and the joy of being desired. Most of all I want her to know that together we are strong, unique, two souls that have merged to become one perfect union.

You don't want much, do you? Do you think she can give you that?

Yes, of course. She's free and mature.

"Oh no, the wolf ate the duck," Cat exclaimed. "What a mean guy."

Herself snickered.

You know what I mean when I say mature, Jessica told Herself crossly. I want to make her realize she's free to choose any way of life she wants.

What if she wants a mohawk and purple hair?

I'll help her dye it. So there! What do you have against Cat anyway, she asked Herself sternly. Out with it!

You're not who you were, Herself said plaintively. You've changed.

Is that so bad?

I guess not, Herself admitted. You seem a lot happier, even if you are a melted puddle around her. *You* haven't had trouble sleeping for months now.

I'm glad you've accepted it.

Herself sighed. Well, why don't you get in bed with her right now? Come on, let's get this show on the road!

Oh hush up, I don't need you helping my sex drive any. It's hyperactive enough as it is.

"Good for Peter. He got the mean old wolf," Cat observed, sliding down into the bed, her eyes closed. "What are we going to do now, Auntie Jessica?"

"You're going to lie still and listen to some nice music while Auntie Jessica keeps the boogie man away."

"Okay."

"Nighty night. Don't let the bedbugs bite," Jessica said softly, turning off the light. That was what her mother had always said to her.

She changed albums to some quiet music. A softly

played guitar streamed comfortingly around Jessica, through the doorway to Cat's bedroom.

"That's nice," she heard Cat say sleepily.

"Go to sleep," Jessica said gently, but with force. The power of suggestion, she hoped. She stretched out on Cat's couch, ready to turn the record over, if need be.

She hadn't thought about her mother or father for a long time. She had been born when her mother was thirty-seven, her father almost fifty. They had always been elderly to her. They had loved her very much, but in an undemonstrative way. She had never wanted for anything, but the quietness of her parents' home had prevented her from asking friends to her house. Consequently she was rarely asked to other girls' houses. So she made only a few friendships, and they were fleeting.

And then when she was nineteen, her parents had died in an accident. She had grieved, missing the quiet way they had supported her life. But then college and self-discovery and coming of age had put her childhood behind her.

How had she lived so many years in a closet of her own making, hiding most of all from her real self? All those years seemed a haze now. There was only Cat and her life since Cat had come into it. When Cat went out of her life again, *if* Cat went out of her life again, she corrected mentally, she would mark it as another era.

She drifted in a sleepy haze, relaxed by the music. She heard the record turn off. No sound came from Cat's bedroom. She decided she'd take a nap before she risked waking Cat up by checking to see if she was asleep.

171

* * * * *

"Jessica, wake up. Come on, wake up."

"What?" Jessica raised her head, wondering briefly where she was. Cat was bending over her, her hair tousled and body backlit by a light from her bedroom.

Cat sat down next to her, one hand on her shoulder. "You fell asleep on my couch. Aunt Jessica's magic cure had its effect on you too," she said with a soft laugh. "I hope you don't have a crick in your neck."

"What time is it?"

"Time for me to get ready for work. I feel so good, thank you. I really needed to sleep and you helped," Cat said. The warmth of Cat's hand on her shoulder burned into Jessica. For a moment Jessica had thought Cat was waking her up in their mutual bed. For a moment she had arched her body toward Cat, wanting to taste her lips, her mouth, the softness of her neck.

As Jessica tried to gather her composure Cat leaned down, her arms sliding under Jessica for a long tight embrace. "I can't remember ever having a friend like you," Cat whispered into Jessica's ear. "Thank you for being there." Jessica felt the soft swell of Cat's breasts pressing against her own and she trembled. "You're cold," Cat said in concern, sitting up again. "My bed's still warm. Why don't you go get in it and go to sleep again? You must still be sleepy."

Jessica wondered what Cat would do if she sat up and kissed her. Cat's body was on the verge of awareness, Jessica instinctively knew it. If she kissed Cat they would go to bed, Jessica knew that, too.

172

And Cat would regret it immediately afterwards, wondering what had led her to do something so perverted. Cat had to make the first move or she would always feel that Jessica had seduced her.

"Come on, sleepyhead," Cat urged, pulling Jessica to her feet.

In a daze she followed Cat. Wearing only panties she slid between the warm sheets of Cat's bed and let lassitude overtake her.

Cat's aroma surrounded her. The pillows smelled of her hair, the sheets of her body. Would Cat lie in her bed tonight and smell Jessica and wonder why the scent comforted her so? Or would she change the sheets before she slept in them?

She listened to the soft noises of Cat showering and then drying her hair, sliding her closet open stealthily. Jessica kept her breathing steady. This is the most erotic thing I've ever done, she told Herself. Sleeping in the bed of the woman I love.

It is pretty hot, Herself admitted.

Not hot, keep your mind out of the gutter. It's erotic. There's a difference.

Considering the state of your nether parts, my dear, Herself replied sarcastically, I don't see any difference.

She sighed deeply. Yes, isn't it wonderful?

"Did I wake you, I'm sorry," Cat said quietly, standing next to the bed.

"No, you didn't. I'm just dozing. Your bed is very warm."

"Electric mattress. It's imported from New Zealand and incredibly self-indulgent."

"Ummm-hmmm. You're leaving. I'll go home now," Jessica said, sitting up. Cat pressed her back

173

into the bed, her hands warm on Jessica's bare shoulders.

"Go to sleep."

"Yes, Aunt Cat." As Cat shut off the bathroom light and walked to the door, Jessica hoisted up on her elbows. The sheets slid to just above her nipples and in the closet door mirrors she could see the sleepy, tousled, wanton picture she made.

"Cat?"

"Yes?" She turned to look at Jessica.

"Are you okay?"

Cat stared at her for a few moments. "Yes. I'm okay." She suddenly flashed a dazzling smile at Jessica. "I'm very okay. See you tonight."

Jessica woke a few hours later, feeling wonderful. She felt sexy and alive, desirable and horny.

She went shopping and tried on a pair of very tight jeans. As she pulled them on she imagined Cat pulling them off. She bought two pair.

While in the lingerie department she saw some body suits, like dancers wore. She tried one on. The fabric did not quite hide the darker color of her nipples. Without a bra, the body suits were extremely provocative and downright naughty. She bought four.

At home she put the turquoise one on and wiggled into the tight jeans. She looked at her reflection. With her new hair style calling attention to her eyes and strong shoulders, she was, in her own humble opinion, very sexy. She had to compromise and put a sweater on — after all it was winter. She still thought she looked pretty sexy.

She pretended to work. At 5:25 she heard the elevator and rapid footsteps hurrying across the foyer.

Cat didn't even go to her place first. She knocked on Jessica's door rapidly.

"You'll never guess," Cat said, grinning. "I could float. This afternoon I called a woman I met at a party the local hotels had for meeting planners and asked if she had some free lunch time this week to talk." She hardly paused for breath. "She not only said yes, she said she hoped I was calling because I was interested in changing jobs."

Cat peeled off her jacket and kicked off her shoes, dropping her briefcase and purse in a pile next to the door. "She wants me to be the corporate account sales manager for their new project, it's going up on the Embarcadero. She said she'd match whatever salary the Regency was paying me with a negotiable bonus package. Since it's a new project we'll have a small staff to begin working on advance bookings, but it will grow to a three or four million dollar budget with a staff of at least ten over the next three years. She said she liked my style and my old boss had said good things about me. She doesn't care that I don't have an MBA! I could fly! I accepted of course."

Jessica smiled broadly. "Congratulations! Talk about cats always landing on their feet! That's terrific. We should celebrate!"

"I'll give my written notice tomorrow after I see Marsha to confirm everything. I am so excited. And it's all thanks to you!"

"To me? I didn't get you a new job," Jessica protested, her heart pounding. Cat was pulsing like a magnet, and Jessica was unable to resist the attraction. She moved slightly closer and her palms started to sweat.

"I went to work this morning feeling like a new

person. Free to do whatever I wanted. I called Marsha up, thinking about what I would say if I were you, and look what happened. She said she could tell I had a lot of enthusiasm. If I'd called her yesterday I'd have sounded flat, desperate. Oh, Jessica, you're wonderful." Cat threw her arms around Jessica, hugging her tightly.

After a long moment, Cat leaned away, her arms still around Jessica and Jessica felt the world stop revolving.

Cat hardly seemed to breathe. Her eyes were glittering with emotion. With a tiny sigh, a breath of confusion, Cat leaned forward and pressed her lips to Jessica's and then buried her face in Jessica's hair.

Without thinking, without breathing, Jessica pressed her lips to Cat's neck, to her ear, to her hair. NOW, Herself said. NOW. Energy pounded in her ears. Hormones exploded. She saw flashing lights. NOW. Do it NOW. Her hands caressed Cat's back eloquently. Cat tensed.

"Jessica?" Cat exhaled breathily. "What are you doing to me?"

"What do you think I'm doing?" Jessica asked in a daze, her lips feathering over the line of Cat's jaw. She felt Cat shudder.

"I don't know . . . I, Jessica," Cat said incoherently. "Oh," she murmured as Jessica kissed her lips.

Jessica gently touched her lips to Cat's, then kissed the corners of her mouth. She was going too fast. Warning bells were ringing in her mind. But Cat's mouth opened and with a gasp she invited Jessica's tongue to explore her, their mouths sharing wetness. Tipping Cat's head back, Jessica explored her thoroughly and then retreated, inviting Cat to follow.

Cat followed. Murmuring between their pressed lips, Cat tasted the recesses of Jessica's mouth. Her hands slid under Jessica's sweater, caressing Jessica's skin through the thin body suit. Slowly, hesitatingly, Cat's fingers crept up Jessica's side, to the soft swell where her breast merged with her ribs, then her hand closed on Jessica's swollen and erect nipple.

They both gasped and Cat broke the kiss, pushing away from Jessica violently.

"I'm sorry, I don't know what made me do that," Cat said, as if she were choking for breath, covering her face with her hands. "I don't know what's wrong with me."

"There's nothing wrong with you," Jessica murmured. She moved slowly toward Cat. "You did what you wanted to do."

"No, Jessica, really, I didn't mean to . . ." Cat said, flushing bright red. She looked at Jessica, aghast.

"Why did you touch me that way?"

"I don't know," Cat said, backing away. "I think I should go."

"Why did you touch me that way?" Jessica asked again, her voice soft with desire, her body burning with love and fever. "You can't shock me, Cat. Tell me."

"I — you kissed me and . . . I — it felt right."

"It felt right to me, too," Jessica whispered. "Every part of me thought it felt right." She stood between Cat and the door, so close to Cat that her breasts almost brushed Cat's folded arms.

Cat swayed slightly. "I don't know what to do, Jessica."

Jessica decided to risk everything. "Do whatever you feel is right. If you leave I won't follow you. I'll wait for you to come back. If you stay. . . ." She swallowed and couldn't go on. Her mouth was dry with want and fear, her throat tight with the words of love she longed to say.

Cat dropped her arms. "Tell me what to do," she whispered, her eyes glazed.

"No. You decide what you want to do," Jessica said in a low, intense voice. "It's your life. Your choice. Never let us misunderstand that."

Cat closed her eyes and her hands went gently to Jessica's face, then her throat. Jessica controlled her gasp of happiness as Cat's hands slid under her sweater, over her shoulders, pushing it back until it slid to the floor.

Cat seemed mesmerized by Jessica's shoulders. Her hands caressed them, from the line of Jessica's collarbone, to her upper arms where Cat brushed against the sides of Jessica's breasts. Opening her eyes, Cat stepped forward. Her lips parted and she brushed them over Jessica's, then they descended.

Her lips pushed away the fabric covering Jessica's shoulders. And Cat's lips went further, kissing Jessica through the thin nylon of the body suit. Without hesitation Jessica pulled it off her shoulders, sliding her arms free. The top peeled slowly down Jessica's body, and the tops of her breasts became available to Cat's seeking lips.

I'm going to come when she takes my breasts in her mouth, I can feel it, Jessica murmured in her mind. I think I may faint. She leaned back against the door, her knees wobbling.

The lips she'd wanted to touch her for so long slowly kissed the sides of her breast, then poised over the bare nipples. Jessica held her breath and then groaned as Cat's warm mouth covered her, pulling her into her mouth, teasing her nipple between her teeth. Jessica shook with the force of a fierce, lightninged orgasm.

"Did I hurt you?" Cat whispered in concern. "I don't know what to do."

"No, no, you're making me crazy, don't stop," Jessica moaned and Cat seemed to explode into fire. She began pulling her clothes off, stopping between buttons and zippers to caress Jessica.

Jessica couldn't move. Her vision went hazy as Cat stood naked before her. She wanted to reach out, to touch, fondle, caress, taste, but her body wouldn't obey her.

Cat pulled her to the floor amid her discarded clothing. She leaned over Jessica, kissing her lips, her nose, her forehead, then tantalizing her breasts with teasing nibbles and warm kisses. "Tell me what to do to you," Cat whispered. "I'll do it. Anything you want." Her tongue trailed over Jessica's lips.

"Undress me, please," Jessica said, trembling. "I want to feel you against me."

Cat slowly peeled Jessica's jeans away, and then the body suit, inch by inch, her hips moving against Jessica's thigh as she gorged herself on Jessica's breasts.

Jessica was moving back against Cat, quivering, shuddering. She felt fire in her fingertips. Electricity prickled across her shoulder blades, then surged down her legs.

"I want to touch you there," Cat groaned.

"Please," she said, in a tight voice. "Please."

Cat parted her and groaned. Her body went rigid and then shook as Jessica opened her legs so that Cat could touch her more completely. Cat's fingers burned through Jessica's flesh, touching, stroking. Jessica held her breath, feeling she would explode from the beating of her heart.

"A little higher . . . Oh." Jessica gasped and everything went purple, blue, then black for a dozen heartbeats. As she became aware of the world again, she realized Cat was sobbing, her hand still cupping Jessica's center.

"What's wrong?" Jessica pulled Cat's head against her breasts. "That was wonderful."

"How can you be so beautiful to me?" Cat sobbed. "Why are you being so kind?"

Jessica lay there for a moment, in a sort of shock. She finally rolled over onto her side, putting Cat's arms around her, pressing the length of her body to the length of Cat's.

"Do you honestly think I opened myself, lying here on the cold floor, gasping in orgasmic pleasure, to be kind to you?"

"Then why are you doing it? I've never done this before, but I think I've always wanted to. Who are you that you can be so good to me?" The brown eyes glowed with feeling.

"I am who I've always been. I'm Jessica. And I love you." She kissed Cat's wet eyes. "I love everything about you. I've been aware of you, thinking about you, mooning over you ever since we

180

went out to dinner the very first time." She smiled in sudden sureness. "What do you have to say to that?"

"I don't believe you," Cat said softly, with a slow smile of wonder. "Convince me. Convince me this isn't just a figment of my overwrought imagination."

"I feel every beat of your heart in my own heart. I feel the tears in your eyes in my own eyes. When you look at me, touch me, talk to me, I see you, feel you, hear you deep within myself, as if you were the very center of me."

"Oh," Cat breathed with a shy smile. She sat up suddenly, and pulled her knees to her chest. Jessica sat up too. "I don't mean to sound like a silly schoolgirl. I just can't believe that you love me — you. I admire you so much, but I never thought you cared much for me in anything but a kind of professional capacity," Cat said seriously.

"I can't believe I was so good at hiding my feelings."

"It never occurred to me. I knew I felt more for you than any friend I'd ever had. I felt as if you were my sister, except I couldn't take you for granted." Her gaze, direct and honest, burned into Jessica. "I found myself admiring your body, but I told myself it was just aesthetics." She smiled beautifully. Jessica felt as if the sun had come out. "This feels so right. I want to make love with you passionately. It's never been this strong before. I'm not afraid."

"Afraid of what?"

"Of anything, not with you. I don't care what anybody or anything thinks. I want to make love with you."

181

"Well, I'm getting cold," Jessica said. "Let's go to bed, shall we?"

"Yes," Cat breathed. "Let's."

Jessica lay back on her pillows while Cat rested her head on Jessica's shoulder, one hand lazily caressing her breasts.

"In one afternoon, in one second, you made my world come together. I've always felt like a tourist in my own life," Cat said with a gentle laugh.

Jessica let Cat's warmth flow over her. "Why is that?" Jessica asked softly.

"There was no you." Cat's voice broke and she burst into tears again.

Cat stopped crying almost immediately and relaxed into the circle of Jessica's arm. Jessica waited for Cat to talk, knowing she would when she was ready.

Instead of the soft voice Jessica expected, she heard a quiet snore and realized that Cat had fallen asleep. She guessed it was a kind of compliment. At least Cat felt comfortable and safe. Jessica was warm and comfortable and safe, too, so she joined Cat in sleep.

TWELVE
Victory

The light had completely gone when Jessica surfaced out of a deep, completely still sleep. She was aware of Cat's body, and one hand that was following the contours of her breasts, pausing to circle her nipples. As she stretched and shifted her position, her nipples tightened and Cat's hand came to a halt.

"Don't stop," Jessica whispered. The hand resumed its teasing and after what seemed hours, Cat began stroking her, lower, lower, until her fingers tangled teasingly in Jessica's pubic hair. She shifted her position and playfully pushed Cat's hand away.

She lay on her side and stared into Cat's eyes for a long while, stroking her face, pushing her hair back. Cat's mouth invited a kiss and Jessica obliged, slowly, carefully, thoroughly.

At last her mouth caressed Cat's velvet and satin shoulders, at last her lips circled the pink swells that graced Cat's full breasts. At last, she was making Cat moan with pleasure and expectation. She made soft sounds of passion as she kissed the swell of Cat's abdomen, descending until she felt Cat open to her.

She heard Cat cry out through the muffling of thighs over her ears. Jessica savored the first taste of her, knowing Cat would come quickly. Thrusting deeply, Jessica clasped Cat's hips to her, wanting to make this first time memorable.

Cat arched and collapsed, her body going limp and Jessica raised her head briefly, then returned, this time exploring each fold and ripple, journeying through Cat, over and over. The pleasure of it, listening to Cat's groans and encouragements, made Jessica break out in a cold sweat.

Higher and higher she took Cat, until they seemed to be floating above the world, vitally locked to each other. Cat quivered, then spasmed and went limp, and Jessica clambered over her to take Cat in her arms.

"I love you, I love you," Jessica whispered. "I've never loved anyone like this. You must believe me."

"I do. I do believe you, Jessica. Let me catch my breath," Cat whispered back. She shivered and hugged Jessica, then lay still.

There was a long comfortable silence and Jessica wondered what Cat was thinking.

"Have there been very many?"

Jessica blinked in surprise. She hadn't expected Cat to ask her that question so soon.

"Yes," she said honestly. "Until I met you my idea of a great relationship was to have a woman in every city I went to. But at about the same time I met you, I began to wonder about it all. Then there was you. And nothing but you would satisfy. I haven't been with anyone since I went to San Antonio and that was a long, long time ago."

"What's her name?"

"Who?"

"The one in San Antonio."

"Marilyn. We're still in touch."

"Oh."

"We agreed that last time to be friends, not lovers. And after that I burned my little black book."

"You really did play the field, didn't you?" Cat observed.

Jessica heard a little bitterness in her voice. Holding Cat in her arms made Jessica fearless. She wanted to tell her everything.

"Yes, I did. But that's not the worst part. Not only was I loving them and leaving them, like some wayward sailor, I even pretended that the fact that they were all women was because it was easier that way, not because I was a lesbian."

"You're not a — a lesbian?" Cat raised her face, a look of startled confusion in her brown eyes.

"I wasn't officially, in my own mind, that is, until this summer, until I realized I was falling in love with you. I had to admit it to myself. But I've always been a lesbian. There have never been any men. I've never wanted men."

185

"I don't think I've ever wanted a woman, not that I've ever realized. I don't know," Cat said slowly. "The last thing I remembered from when I went to sleep was you framed in the doorway of my bedroom. And ever since this morning when I woke up, my life has seemed real. Everything I do seems real," Cat said, settling into Jessica's arms again. "I've never felt this close to anybody before. And — and sex has never been that good —" Jessica saw a delicate blush creep into Cat's cheeks. "— or that intimate."

"I didn't dare hope for this," Jessica said with a gentle laugh. She was overwhelmed with joy. A loud rumble went through her stomach. "Are you hungry?"

"Am I hungry," Cat said suggestively, her eyes full of dangerous laughter and shy determination.

Jessica went limp, all over. "What are you suggesting?" she breathed out finally.

"I don't know what to do," Cat said slowly, just above a whisper, "but I want to do what you did to me, I want to learn to make you feel as good as you made me feel. Tell me what to do," she said earnestly.

Jessica quivered. "I've never been anyone's teacher in this way before," she said. "I'll try."

"Please, Jessica, I want to," Cat said seriously, sensuously. "Do you like this?" she asked, one finger softly stroking Jessica.

"Yes. Imagine what you would like me to do to you and just do that to me. I'm sure, oh —" Jessica gasped as Cat slid into her.

"Sure what?"

"Sure you'll do just fine," Jessica managed to say. She was beyond words. Cat trailed her hair over

Jessica's body, still slowly stroking her as she knelt slowly between Jessica's thighs. Jessica held her breath as Cat slowly bent, stroking Jessica's pubic hair, her eyes glowing.

"You're beautiful," Cat whispered as her lips kissed Jessica softly. Her groan mixed with Jessica's and Jessica felt tears in her eyes. She burned with elation. She wound her fingers into the curls of blonde hair which brushed the softness of her inner thighs. There would be no one else after this, no way.

"Thank you," Jessica finally said, much later. She felt as if her bones had turned to jelly. There was no strength left in her. Cat kissed the trickle of tears down the side of Jessica's face.

"I made you cry," she said. "No one has ever cried for me before. I could get used to this."

They made tuna fish sandwiches and sat crosslegged on the couch.

"We're eating fish. Should we be drinking red wine or white?" Cat asked, smiling as she ate.

"I'm not sure canned tuna qualifies as fish," Jessica said, giggling, "and besides, I've never believed those rules anyway. I drink what I want, when I want."

"I certainly hope so," Cat said slyly, with a nervous giggle.

"You surprise me every moment," Jessica said softly. She looked at Cat. "I've been biding my time, waiting, afraid to approach you because I was sure you wouldn't accept a relationship with me. There was Paul, you know. And you talked about men a lot."

"Paul, dear Paul. Stupid Paul. Macho Paul. Paul was the epitome of the men I chose to make myself miserable with. I was never interested in getting married. I always wanted to have the kind of sex you read about in books," she finished.

Then her eyes widened, as if a new thought had struck her. "I practically jumped into Paul's arms last summer. I let him stay the night again for the first time — it was the night you cut your foot. I was so, well, hot and bothered." Cat swept her hair off her neck and thought for a moment, blushing. "I really made him work, but I wasn't ever satisfied. Not until today."

"I wasted a lot of time, but you put up quite a smoke screen," Jessica said, wanting Cat to know everything she'd been feeling.

"I honestly don't know what I would have done if you'd approached me sooner. In New York, we seemed so close and I never even suspected you might love me. I only knew that I wanted to spend time with you more than anyone else, including the jerk at the bar."

"Oh, my love." Jessica lifted Cat's hair from her shoulders and let it ripple through her hand. She'd been longing to do that for ages.

"I like the way you say that," Cat said, leaning her head against Jessica's hand. "I remember how disappointed I was my first time. Losing my virginity was not exactly pleasant. How was your first time?"

"Fabulous. Her name was Phoebe. Of course, it was just simpler that way, you understand. I wasn't a lesbian or anything like that."

Cat laughed. "We should get medals for how well we've deceived ourselves for so long."

"I'm beginning to think so," Jessica said. "It's

taken me all my life to see the vision. There's no turning back now."

"I couldn't turn back." Cat pushed aside their plates and cuddled happily in Jessica's arms.

"Wait here a second," Jessica said. She kissed Cat on the tip of her nose and slid out from under her. "Be right back," she called, digging into the very back of her closet.

"What's this?" Cat asked as Jessica handed her the Bloomingdale's bag, a trifle crumpled and dog-eared. "You bought these way back then? For me?"

"For you and no one but you."

"I'll show you my runway walk from my modelling days," Cat said, her face flushed with pleasure. "I love these slippers."

"You'd better hurry up with the modelling show," Jessica said, her voice getting husky. "You're not going to wear that for very long."

* * * * *

Every day was heaven. Cat gave her notice, and wrote her letter to the Board of Directors about Jim Barton. At night, Jessica marvelled at how much *she* was learning about lovemaking from Cat. They went out to dinner and stared into each other's eyes for long periods of time, as if neither could believe the other existed.

One Friday night they were cuddling on Jessica's couch, Cat in the corner and Jessica sitting between her legs, leaning back on her chest toboggan style. Flicking through the channels, they immediately rejected *Fantasy Island* and Jessica tried the other stations.

"Wait," Cat said. "Go back, what was that?"

"It's Briggs, the illustrious Senator Briggs. What is he doing on public television?"

The picture shifted and Cat laughed. "Debating Harvey Milk! I want to watch this."

"I didn't know you were following the Briggs Initiative," Jessica said.

"I wasn't, not really, I've just always thought Harvey Milk was a neat guy. And until real recently, I didn't think the Briggs Initiative would ever apply to me. I wasn't a homosexual then." There was laughter in Cat's voice.

"But it's a precedent," Jessica said earnestly. "It's actually a repression of free thought and free speech."

"Okay, okay. I didn't understand it quite that way a week ago, but I understand it perfectly now. Isn't he something?"

"Harvey?"

"Yes. I wish I had his poise, his sureness that he's right."

They watched him refute the Senator's arguments. He wasn't cool. He didn't use flawless logic delivered with cutting dignity. He was logical, but passionately so. He didn't argue constitutionality, but the logic of human rights. He came back to one point. His people shall be free. And everyone who wasn't a middle-class straight male was one of Harvey's people. He tried to speak for them all.

Jessica sighed happily as Cat kissed the top of her head and hugged her periodically. When the debate was over a Tyrone Power swashbuckler movie came on and on impulse, Jessica rolled over and unbuttoned Cat's blouse.

"Oh, fie," Cat protested. "Why, what are you doing? How can a helpless maid withstand such force?" Cat unhooked her bra and shoved Jessica's hands under her blouse. "Why, how you push yourself on me."

Jessica giggled. "I shall take thee to bed, wench."

"Oh, no, I beg of thee," Cat cried dramatically, jumping off the couch. "Do not force me," she said as she ran into the bedroom, shedding her clothes along the way. Jessica heard her body go thump on the bed. "You have overwhelmed me," she called.

Jessica walked slowly to the bedroom. Cat was already under the covers, naked. Jessica stopped in the doorway. I feel as if I'm in a state of grace when I'm with her, she told Herself. How can she be so very much everything I dreamed about?

"I love you," she whispered, walking to the bed.

"Prove it," Cat whispered sensuously, all her laughter gone. "I'm yours, Jessica."

They said nothing more to each other than their own language of interchange, murmurs of ecstasy, groans of deepfelt want. The world was wet and salty sweet, inflamed and charged with electricity. Legs entwined arms entwined legs. Mouths were thirsty and drank sweetness. Emptinesses were filled.

* * * * *

Election day was Cat's first day at her new job, and Jessica met her to celebrate at the Italian restaurant where they had first had dinner. Cat chattered away about her new staff, her new boss and Jessica sat in the glow of her enthusiasm.

"It's great to be working on a new project. You don't have any shortcomings to gloss over. There are three convention planners on the architectural board for the hotel, so we should have perfect meeting space."

"It's amazing to think your job could be so ideal after the crud you went through with Jim Barton," Jessica said.

"Hey — I forgot to tell you! Marsha heard from a trusted source — you would not believe this woman's grapevine — that Jim Barton has just been transferred back to corporate. He was promoted to vice president of disappearing markets." She was grinning happily.

"A promotion?" Jessica was incredulous. "That hardly seems fair."

"Sorry." Cat laughed. "It's an insider joke. It actually means he's been transferred to a position that sounds better but is organizationally less important. No subordinates. Marsha said no one will say why."

"But we know, don't we?" Jessica said, smiling back at Cat.

"I'm just about finished," Cat said a few minutes later, pushing the last of her fettucini around on her plate. "I don't want to get too full. A full stomach makes me sleepy and I don't particularly want to go to sleep tonight. At least not right away," she said, wiggling her eyebrows at Jessica.

"You darling," Jessica said, reaching across the

table. She linked her fingers with Cat's. "Have I told you recently how much I adore you?"

"No. At least not since this morning," Cat teased. She looked at their linked fingers. "Aren't you afraid people might stare at us?" she asked Jessica quietly.

"A little, but I want to touch you," Jessica said softly. She released Cat and then realized that the man and woman at the next table were staring at them. The couple looked away when Jessica returned their stare.

"They looked at us as if we were insects," Cat muttered.

They finished their dinner quickly and walked home, mostly in silence.

"Well," Cat said, finally. "You tried."

"Tried what?"

"To make a statement."

"I wasn't trying to make a statement. I wanted to touch you," Jessica repeated. "If they can't handle it, that's their problem."

"I can't handle it," Cat said slowly. "I mean I can, but I thought I wasn't going to have any problems."

"Someday it'll be okay, I know it," Jessica said. "Let's watch the returns and see what happened with Briggs. I have this feeling that it's not going to pass, that people just don't believe that gay and lesbian people are after their children's bodies."

"I hope you're right," Cat said doubtfully.

Most of the local coverage was devoted to the Briggs Initiative — defeating it meant a lot to San Francisco. By the time the votes were tallied, two-thirds of the voters said that they didn't think that job discrimination against gays was right and so they voted 'no' — and proposition six failed. The local news reported parties all over San Francisco's gay community.

"Let's go, Jessica," Cat said suddenly. "I want to be part of the victory. It's what I am now."

"Are you sure?" Jessica asked quietly. God, it took me forever to get used to being a lesbian. How did she come to terms with it so quickly?

"Yes. It feels right. That's where I belong, in that community. Let's go join the celebration! We won," Cat declared, with growing excitement. "A month ago I didn't belong to anything. Now I belong to all those people and the entire movement. I *want* to belong."

"Okay," Jessica said, jumping up. "Let's go find out what's out there for us!"

Cat kissed her enthusiastically and they changed and caught a cab to the Castro district where Harvey Milk was supervisor. It didn't take the driver long to find a neighborhood bar filled with people.

"This is great," Cat said in Jessica's ear as they squeezed toward the bar. They found a spot and ordered drinks and Jessica felt Cat's arm slide around her waist. She put her arm around Cat's shoulders. They were among friends. They had nothing to hide from anyone. Jessica felt drunk already, drunk on freedom and happiness.

"I feel wonderful," she whispered to Cat, and she kissed her softly on the corner of her mouth.

Cat kissed her back. "I think we shouldn't stay too late," she murmured suggestively. "There are a few things I'd like to get done when we get home."

"Such as," Jessica prompted.

Cat's response was drowned in sudden shouts and

194

people all over the bar stomping their feet and applauding. Harvey Milk had just walked in. Standing on tiptoe, Jessica looked at the man who inspired her with so much hope.

Harvey Milk was not a tall man, not an imposing figure. But he had that quality of being a man of the people. There was an aura about him that attracted everyone, including Jessica. She wanted to bask in his courageous light for a moment, take a piece of it away with her. He gradually gravitated to where she and Cat were standing, arms around each other, and suddenly Jessica found her courage.

"Supervisor Milk, I want to thank you for your commitment," she said. What a dumb thing to say, she thought. Cat seemed tongue-tied.

"Did you vote today?" he asked, with a smile of polite interest.

They both nodded silently. "I'm grateful for what you've done for us," Cat said, after a gulp. She squeezed Jessica. "You've changed our lives, a lot of people's lives."

"Thank you very much," he said sincerely. "That's what I want, for people to care." Someone else attracted his attention and Jessica was overwhelmed with the excitement of having met a man she felt was going to make a significant, long-term impact on the gay rights movement. She felt the hope of it in her soul.

People called for a speech and Harvey Milk was coaxed up onto a bar stool. "I don't want to make a speech," he said when the bar fell respectfully quiet. "I want to celebrate." He raised his beer. "Here's to homogeneity!" He grinned. "Look it up," was all he said.

Much later that night, Cat did the few things she'd wanted to get done and then Jessica was pressing her down into the bed.

"Your turn to lie back and enjoy it," she said huskily. "You make me so happy. I'm going to love you any way you like."

"Yes, Jessica," Cat breathed.

"Do you like this?" she asked as her mouth alternately caressed one beautiful, erect nipple, then the other.

"Yes."

"More?"

"Yes."

"Touching?"

"Yes."

"Lower?"

"Yes."

"Here?" Jessica said with a sigh of anticipation.

"Yes."

Jessica parted Cat with her tongue. She knew she was going to cry while she loved Cat but she couldn't help it. Cat trembled and kept murmuring "Yes." Jessica immersed her tongue in Cat's taste, Cat's feel, Cat's softness. She felt Cat gather herself slowly, tighter and tighter until her entire body flexed and fluttered in ecstasy.

Jessica didn't want to move her mouth. It fit perfectly into Cat. She wanted to put her arms around Cat's hips and just lie there, but she was sobbing too hard to breathe properly and finally she lifted her head.

"Darling," Cat whispered, "what's wrong?"

"Nothing, nothing's wrong. I'm so happy, Cat. I love you, Cat, I love you so much," Jessica said in a jumble. "I don't know what I've done to deserve this kind of joy."

"I was just asking myself that question," Cat said. "I feel silly and over-romantic, but I feel as if fate has pushed us together — that I was meant to be with you."

"It's spooky," Jessica said. "And wonderful."

"Wunnerful, wunnerful," Cat said with a laugh. "Where are you going?" she asked as Jessica suddenly got out of bed.

"Hang on a second." Jessica swore as she stubbed her toe on her desk. She turned on the light and found her dictionary. Standing in the door of her office she read to Cat.

"Homogeneity. Comparable. Equivalent. Having no discordant elements."

"Nice word," Cat murmured when Jessica returned to bed.

"Sure is. A word to live by."

They slept on it.

* * * * *

The following evening, after what Cat called an I-missed-you-all-day-roll-in-the-hay, Cat was making dinner and Jessica was watching *Bugs Bunny* when Jessica's doorbell rang. Jessica grabbed a robe while Cat dashed into the bedroom for her clothes. "Who can it be?" Cat asked as she flew by.

"I've no idea," Jessica said. She belted her robe around her tightly and peeped through the peephole. The hallway was dark, but she could tell it was a woman. She opened the door.

"Roberta!" Jessica was stunned.

"Jessie!" Roberta exclaimed. Jessica recognized the tight red satin pants before Roberta threw her arms around Jessica. "Some guy let me in the building. I wanted to surprise you! It's so good to see you!"

In shock, Jessica stood back and invited Roberta in. She watched in a daze as Roberta carried in a large suitcase. Oh no, she wailed to Herself. What will Cat think? What will I say to Cat? What will I say to Roberta? Herself observed smugly that this situation had been bound to happen someday and Jessica should have thought ahead.

"What are you doing west of the Mississippi?" Jessica asked. She couldn't think of anything else to say.

"Following the path of employment. I got tired of Chicago and decided to come to California. All the disco's are in California, along with the sunshine," Roberta explained, looking around her with interest. "You look great."

"So do you. Uh, why don't I go get dressed," Jessica said, aware of Roberta's sexual scrutiny.

"If you think you must," Roberta answered.

Just then the bedroom door opened and Cat came in, dressed. Jessica knew Cat must have heard their conversation.

She performed perfunctory introductions. Cat smiled and shook hands and seemed to wait for Jessica to say more, to explain her relationship to Jessica. Jessica was losing control of the situation.

Roberta looked at Jessica again and flushed. "I think I arrived at a bad time. I wanted to surprise you. Maybe I should come back later."

Jessica saw Cat take a deep breath. Her eyes bored into Jessica's, commanding her to say *something.* Jessica's mouth opened and closed slowly. You're doing fish imitations again, Herself said. "No, don't be silly."

"Oh," Roberta said, looking from Cat to Jessica. "Are you, I mean —"

"We're neighbors," Cat said coolly. Jessica felt Cat's rage and hurt like heat from an open oven. "I'll be going now so you can visit with your friend," she told Jessica sweetly, too sweetly.

"There's no need," Jessica began.

"Oh I have scads of housework to do and grocery shopping, of course. See you later, maybe."

Cat smiled and said nice to meet you to Roberta and then she left. Jessica heard the too-quiet click of Cat's door on the other side of the foyer. She sank down on her sofa.

"Wow," Roberta admired. "She's beautiful. And how convenient. I wouldn't mind spending a few hours between those legs."

Jessica's head shot up, and she blushed a furious red. "She's not available," she told Roberta in a quavering voice. "We're lovers, we're together."

"Sorry," Roberta snapped. "Why didn't you say so?"

Yes, indeed, Herself asked, why didn't you say so when Cat was here?

"I guess my surprise was a big mistake."

"I am glad to see you, but I can't —"

"Oh, I understand," Roberta said bitterly. She pushed her hands into the pockets of her jacket. "Don't call us, we'll call you. Story of my life."

"I'm sorry. I never expected to see you again," Jessica said in a quiet voice.

"I never pegged you for a one-woman woman,

199

Jessie," Roberta said, turning her back on her. "I've got some other friends to see, so I guess I'll be going."

"I am sorry, Roberta. We had a very good time."

"I was looking forward to more," she said.

"I can't."

"Tied you down, has she?"

"No! I tied myself down. I love her and I wouldn't hurt her for the world," Jessica said passionately. Herself commented that she had a strange way of showing it. And she was saying it to the wrong person.

"I see. Well, I guess this is goodbye, Jessica. It was nice knowing you."

Jessica wanted to cry, but she merely shook Roberta's hand gravely.

She hurriedly changed into jeans and a sweater, and then went across to Cat's door. There was no answer to her knock. She didn't have a key because there had never been a need.

They hadn't talked about living together, although the words had trembled on Jessica's lips several times. It was too soon. Cat could still find that life with her wasn't what she wanted. Herself observed that Cat didn't seem to be having any problems with the situation. The hesitancy seemed to all be on Jessica's side.

She went back home and sat down in the living room in a stupor. Why hadn't she said "Roberta, this is my lover, Cat Merrill?" But no, she had introduced Cat like an acquaintance, as if she were a one-night stand.

"Fool, fool, fool," she called Herself, over and over. Herself refused to take the blame. She went walking in the Park, looking for Cat. There were a lot of pretty blonde women, but none of them was a very special pretty blonde, short, brown-eyed, and adorable in every way.

Cat wasn't at O'Malley's, or the corner grocery, or the pizza place. Jessica walked and walked, getting more and more upset. She was to blame. She went back to Cat's door and knocked, but there was no answer. She tried the knob, but the door was truly locked.

Now you've done it, Herself commented. You finally tell her you love her and she's already dumped you.

She hasn't dumped me!

She never said she loved you, did she?

Well, no, but she does. She just doesn't know how much, yet.

Dream on. She's decided you're just a slut and she doesn't want to sleep with you again.

No, no!

Well, what would you think if you saw Cat with an airhead disco fiend like Roberta, in those tight pants and even tighter shirt?

I'd think she was easy, Jessica admitted. I'd think she'd sure slept around, and not with very much discrimination.

She cried until she slept.

The next morning her eyes were swollen and puffy and her nose was horribly red. I look like death warmed over, she thought. She wanted Cat to come home from work so they could talk. She had never meant to love Cat so much that being apart like this would hurt so much — it had just happened. It was almost dark when she heard footsteps and a key in the door across from hers.

She threw open her door and Cat turned from her own door to look at her.

"Cat, I don't know what to say. I'm sorry." Jessica tried to control her shaking voice and shaking hands. She wanted to talk about this calmly.

"What for?" Cat asked softly. She turned and walked into her apartment. Jessica followed slowly. "You only love me. You never talked about anything more."

"Love is everything," Jessica said, somewhat incoherently. Tears trickled down her face. "I don't know why I was suddenly afraid. I was afraid to say 'this is my lover.' "

"What the hell are you afraid of, Jessica? You've had longer than I have to get used to the idea of being gay, but you won't go all the way, will you? You're so damned cautious." She whirled around and flashed at Jessica, "I won't be your mistress, damn it! I won't let you screw me every night and then fade into the background whenever anyone else is around! I think you'd better go. I have a busy week ahead of me and I need some sleep." Cat turned her back on Jessica.

"Can we talk tomorrow night?" Jessica whispered.

Cat nodded but said nothing.

Jessica backed out of Cat's living room and shut the door. She thought she heard a stifled sob, but knew it was just her imagination. Cat just didn't love her.

THIRTEEN
Beginnings

Jessica hung out of her window all evening, watching for Cat.

Herself was thoroughly disgusted with the entire situation. This is really undignified.

I don't care. I have to see her.

Well, then at least get some work done while you wait. How do you expect to keep a roof over your head if you don't work? Herself was convinced someone had to be practical about this whole situation.

I'll work tomorrow. Or next week. I just can't work right now.

The sun had long since set when a bus pulled up at the corner, and a petite figure in a black suit got off and walked slowly up the street.

She wiped her eyes on her shirt. She had to talk to her. She waited until she heard Cat's footsteps in the hall, then her key in her door. Jessica opened her door and stared across the hallway.

Cat slowly turned from her open door, staring back at Jessica. With a deep sigh, she held out her arms.

Jessica flew across the corridor, and flung herself into Cat's arms. "I'm sorry, I'm sorry," she sobbed, over and over.

"God, I'm sorry, too. I tried to forget about you, but I couldn't," Cat breathed.

"I've been beside myself," Jessica said, her breathing still shaky. She pulled her head back and looked into Cat's eyes. They were bloodshot.

"So have I," Cat said, wearily. "Come on in and let me change. Then we can talk."

Jessica sat down on Cat's couch, listening to the rustle of her clothing and the sounds of her moving around in her bedroom. Cat joined her on the couch, wearing jeans and a T-shirt.

"I'm so sorry, Cat," Jessica began, but Cat reached out for her hand and shushed her.

"No, I'm sorry. Let me just get this out, okay?" Cat said as Jessica tried to interrupt her. "I knew you were caught off guard by that woman showing up. And we hadn't talked about 'us.' We hadn't talked about 'us' because I didn't want to. Sex with you is great. It's the best I've ever had. I felt great. I could go to work, go to bed with you, and my life would go on pretty much as before. No risks, no dangers, no complications."

Cat fell silent, then slowly stroked the hand she was holding as she went on. "When you introduced me to Roberta I suddenly saw the whole picture. I suddenly realized that I could go on characterizing our relationship as completely sexual and put it down to some peculiar sex need I had. But then I realized I was jealous. I was jealous of her and jealous that you'd been with other women. I wanted you all for myself. Not just for sex, but for keeps." Cat swallowed and took a deep breath. "I realized I loved you. And I wasn't sure you loved me."

"But I told you I did. I do love you," Jessica protested.

"You said it while we were making love. I'm sorry, Jessica, but I thought you must say that to all of us," she choked, then swallowed. "All your women."

Jessica took Cat's face in her hands. She gazed into Cat's eyes. "I've never said those words before in my life."

"I believe you," Cat said after a moment. "So why did you introduce me like that, like I was some woman you picked up?"

"That's not what I was doing," Jessica protested. She let go of Cat.

"You acted as if you were ashamed of me," Cat said gently. "At least that's how I saw it."

"I'm not ashamed of you. I'm ashamed of myself. I was ashamed that you were seeing what I was before I met you."

"You're kidding."

"No, I looked at Roberta and she's very nice, but I treated her like a sex object when I knew her. I didn't care about her brains, only her body. She may have brains, but I don't know. I couldn't bear you to see how easy I was before. I let Roberta pick me up."

"That's in the past, isn't it? We have the future to think about."

Cat went to make some tea and Jessica calmed down, finally. Her head hurt and her eyes stung, but she was at last sure that she and Cat were going to be together. Cat sat down next to her with the cups. They sipped in silence, then Jessica put her cup down. She crept into the circle of Cat's arm and laid her head on Cat's thigh. "I'm sorry about Roberta," she said in a small voice.

"And I'm sorry I got so mad — I surprised myself. I have to get used to this, to you, to us. Look, let's not talk about the future right now. Give ourselves some time, okay?"

Jessica nodded. "We have all the time in the world."

* * * * *

Jessica lay in a very empty and lonely hotel bed in Denver. She was speaking for the next two days. Herself was looking forward to it. Jessica was missing Cat horribly.

It was all Cat's fault, she told Herself crossly. Cat

had kissed her goodbye a few short hours ago, and her kiss had been inviting and wanting.

"There isn't any time," Jessica had gasped. "Because you kept me in bed all afternoon."

"I know. Miss me while you're away?" Cat had asked, her eyes dancing with the delight of driving Jessica to distraction.

"Of course. Kiss me again."

Groaning, she rolled over in bed. She would never get to sleep. She sat up and turned the light on. Fumbling in the pseudo-Queen Anne desk, she found some hotel stationery and an envelope. She made some space to write. It would sure be a hell of a lot more comfortable if I could move this lamp out of the way, Jessica thought to Herself. Herself whined about lack of sleep. But once the pen was in Jessica's hand the words flowed out of her.

I am unable to sleep. Memory comes between me and sleep and I find myself using memory as delightful torment.

Never could I have believed I would love this way. Coolly, remotely, distantly, yes I imagined all of that. But to have lost myself completely, out of control, this I never imagined. To love in such a way that I am sure, despite all the books and poetry to the contrary, that no one has ever loved the way I love you. I am the rings to your Saturn, my love.

I know we agreed to give ourselves time — but please imagine that there is candlelight. Soft music surrounds you and me, alone together. You smile at me over the rim of a wine glass, your face reflecting the golden light. I take your hand and kneel at your side.

This is how I envision it. Thanksgiving Day I was

planning to — I can't wait. Away from you I feel tenfold the wretchedness I feel every moment when you are away from me. I hate the ten minutes it takes you to go to your apartment and pick out your clothes in the morning. I dread that each morning, yet I say nothing because there is really only one solution to it and I have not yet been brave enough to suggest it. My emptiness has become my courage.

If I ramble, you should know it is well after midnight and I am groggy from lack of sleep and tensely exhausted from longing for your smile, your kiss. I had planned that on Thanksgiving I would ask you to be with me. I would ask you to let me be with you, lover and partner, wife and wife.

Perhaps I won't mail this. Or if I do mail it, I'll beat it home and steal it out of the mailbox before you see it. I am so frightened of your answer. I know the honesty and depth of what you feel for me, and my mind says to trust in you.

At the risk of being horribly old-fashioned and dated, my love,

— will you marry me?

She stared down at her neatly printed words. They looked so cold on the paper. She wished there were some way to make the paper warm so that when Cat held it she would know how Jessica was burning.

* * * * *

Jessica's hand was shaking slightly as she dialed Cat's number. You know there's no way she'll have

208

received the letter yet, Herself observed. Calm down. She'll get it Federal Express tomorrow. You promised to call tonight.

"Hello," the soft voice said and Jessica shivered.

"Hi. It's me," she answered.

"Hello me," Cat said. "I miss you."

"Me, too. I mean I don't miss me, I miss you, too," Jessica fumbled. "I don't know why I feel so shy all of a sudden."

"This is the first time we've talked by phone since . . . you know," Cat said. "It's very strange. I hear your voice and I expect you to be right there next to my ear. This black plastic handset isn't a very satisfying substitute."

"I know what you mean."

There was a long silence.

"What are you thinking about?" Cat asked.

"You," Jessica said, her voice a near groan.

"Hurry home," Cat whispered. "I — oh, hurry home."

"I will."

"This phone stuff is for the birds," Cat said. "Let's not get in the habit of talking long-distance."

"Okay. Bye."

"Bye," Cat said and the line went dead.

Jessica managed to get through the second day of her seminar. She had done an adequate job, but she was not about to believe any of the women who told her she had been marvelous.

"Thanks," she said pleasantly to everyone who came up to speak to her after she adjourned the workshop. She had never before wished her participants would leave her alone. There was this and the plane ride to get through. And deep inside, barely locked away, was the knowledge that Cat had received the letter today.

On the plane, she glanced through the newspaper. Nothing particular of interest. Dan White had resigned from the Board of Supervisors, she noted. A step in the right direction. She shut her eyes and ears to the airplane's mechanical intensity. What would Cat's answer be?

Yes, she'll say yes. She loves me. She knows I'm not asking to trap her, but to let her be a part of me so I can be a part of her.

The shuttle from the airport to the hotel district took forever because a 49er game was letting out, swamping the Bayshore Freeway with cars honking horns, turning on their lights. The descending evening was cool and blustery as she sat on her suitcase on a corner, waiting for her cross-town connection home.

Why didn't I tell her she could keep all her furniture? Why didn't I tell her she could have her choice of condos? Why didn't I tell her that if she wanted a baby we could try artificial insemination? Why didn't I tell her she didn't have to answer me right away? She can take her time. A few days, a year. I'll wait until she says yes.

"I can't stand it," she said aloud, startling several people around her. She stepped out into traffic and hailed a cab. She fretted as she sat in the back seat, wishing she were already home, and wishing she would never get home if the answer was no.

Her suitcase gripped tightly, far tighter than necessary, she unlocked the building door and went to the elevator. She pushed the button and slowly, so slowly she wanted to scream, it began its slow journey to the top floor.

The second floor looked as it always did as she rose slowly past it. The third floor came into view, and through the cage's wrought iron bars she saw the flicker of a candle sitting on the floor of the tiny foyer between her and Cat's doors.

Stepping out of the elevator, she set down her suitcase. The candle was the only light, securely held in its holder.

Then she noticed a piece of paper on the floor in front of the candle.

The piece of paper said YES.

Turning slowly, she saw YES taped to the mirror over the tiny table, YES clinging to the walls, YES scattered on the floor. She picked up the candlestick and held it over her head. YES was everywhere.

She wondered now which door Cat was behind, regretting the moments wasted in wondering. Then she saw the paper taped to her door.

YOU GOOSE, it said. WHY ARE YOU OUT THERE WHEN YOU COULD BE IN HERE?

* * * * *

They practiced co-habitating several times that night.

EPILOGUE
The End of the Beginning

On November 27, the Monday after Thanksgiving weekend, Jessica was sequestered in the stacks of Moffit library at Berkeley. She concentrated single-mindedly on her research.

Occasionally she recalled the tenderness and warmth of Cat's love, and with it was the memory of a night spent sobbing out grief and rage over the news from Jonestown, over the helpless anguish of knowing a vital, loving woman she had held in her arms was dead.

It was dark when she left Berkeley, her satchel slung over one shoulder, and she took the BART transbay tube to 19th Street. From there she got on her bus, tired, rubbing her eyes a little. Somebody in the dimness of the bus was crying and she stared out the window to give her her privacy.

"Sorry about the detour, folks," the driver said, addressing Jessica and the other passengers. Jessica looked around her, wondering why they weren't going the usual way. There were only a few people on the bus.

"It's okay," one man answered him. "We're getting off at the march." He put his arm around his companion, who buried his face in his hands. It was a woman several rows back who was crying, helplessly. The other passengers were also subdued, silent.

The bus came into the Castro District and suddenly Jessica saw the lights and people. There were people everywhere, alone, in couples, in trios. Most held candles and they were walking, heads down.

"What is it?" Jessica asked. "What's happening?"

The man raised his head to look at Jessica, opened his mouth and was unable to speak. It was the other man who answered her.

"It's a march for a martyr," he said.

"Who?" Jessica whispered. "I haven't heard the news."

"Harvey's dead. Dan White shot him this morning. Moscone, too."

She whispered a silent no and became unconscious

of time. When the bus stopped and the other passengers got off, she followed them, numb with shock, empty in her grief.

She found a phone booth and dialed home. It rang and rang and in her mind's eye, Jessica could see a note on the door from Cat telling her she was at the march. Somewhere in this crowd Cat needed her, and Jessica desperately needed Cat.

Jessica was surprised she felt nothing. She left the phone booth and walked toward the growing numbers of people. It would be impossible to find Cat, but later, in the warm safety of their home, they would find each other again.

The crowd was large. She filtered through the fringe, getting more to the heart of it. A drum beat began and people lit their candles. Candles were touched from person to person as the flame passed through the crowd until the darkness receded. People with extras handed candles to those without and Jessica murmured an inadequate thank you. The night was filled with flickering lights and the smell of candle wax and burnt matches. She knew she would never forget that smell.

The march went slowly, through the moonlight and candlelight. There were hymns being sung and she sang along when she knew the words. The rest of the time she just walked, lost in thought.

She heard someone ask a man where his anger was, but the man didn't reply. There was no anger. Just tearfulness and heartache.

At first there were just those who started in Castro. Gay men and women, many in couples, holding each other, carrying their candles before them. Kind candlelight illuminated faces tormented with despair and grief. She stopped looking at the faces. The expressions were private — emotion laid bare by shock and anguish.

She saw men with candles dripping wax onto their hands but they didn't seem to notice. She saw lovers, holding each other, crying. The chill of the misty night settled on her hair, her face, but she was only dimly aware of the cold. The sound of weeping joined with the drums, and the march went slowly on.

As they left Castro the crowd began to swell, began to change. Now there were older people, heterosexual couples, all carrying candles. Many were in tears. She thought about Harvey Milk's Homogeneity. Did it take death, pain, suffering to bring people together?

They turned onto Polk, and Jessica looked behind her, back toward Castro. The candles flickered for miles, tiny stars down the length of Market Street as far as she could see, and yet there was only the sound of singing, of footsteps, and the drums. The voices rose and fell like a requiem, so full of sadness that the music seemed to come from the ground itself, laden with passionate grief.

At City Hall, the crowd stopped. And as one, they raised their candles over their heads. Then, a moment of silence.

For an incredible minute, she heard nothing. The emptiness of inner despair carried itself to the air and all was silent and still. There was no breathing, no crying, only the dull roar of traffic on Van Ness two blocks away, and the hiss of melting candlewax.

Then someone began singing "Amazing Grace" and as the crowd began to join in choked, aching voices, she heard a familiar, sweet voice at her side.

215

Somehow, she wasn't surprised to find Cat standing there, singing, her candle raised. She put her arm around Cat's shoulders. When Cat's arm slid around her waist in comfort, Jessica began to cry at last.

In the uncertain hour before morning, near the ending of interminable night, Jessica thought, tears streaming down her face, *will the sun shine on our despair? Will there be an end?*

Other people began to cry again. But Jessica stood still and Cat finally turned to her.

"Nothing really matters, does it?"

"Except you," Jessica said in a raw whisper in her aching throat. "I can't believe he's gone."

"Let's go home," Cat said. "They can't take that away from us."

"Never."

They put the tips of their candles slowly together and the joined flames flared into one bright, comforting light.

Comments from the Author . . .

Harvey Milk was the first martyr of my generation. JFK, Bobby Kennedy, and Dr. King were dead before I was old enough to know they were alive. I have seen them only as shadowy figures on black and white film.

Harvey Milk was no shadow. In doing research for this book, I was appalled by the lack of information about him, his words and his work in standard reference sources, and so I relied heavily on the *San Francisco Chronicle* and the moving, vivid documentary, *The Times of Harvey Milk,* which is available on video cassette now. Keep some tissues handy; I need only hear a few bars of Mark Isham's score for the Candlelight March to get a familiar lump in my throat. Anyone wanting to know more about Harvey Milk and what he stood for should read Randy Shilts's *Mayor of Castro Street.*

To Homogeneity!